YES

Jez Alborough

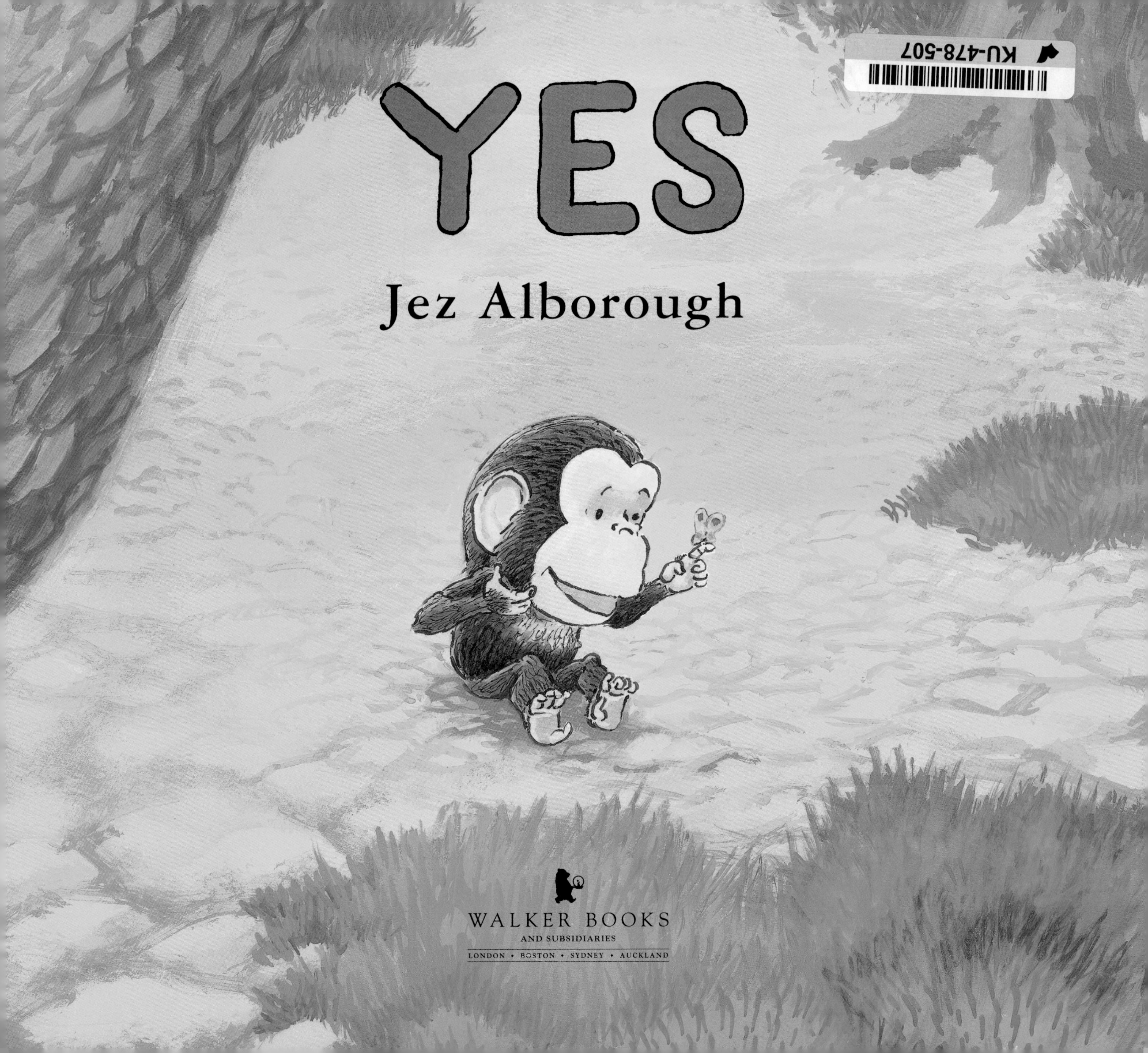

WALKER BOOKS
AND SUBSIDIARIES
LONDON • BOSTON • SYDNEY • AUCKLAND

KU-478-507

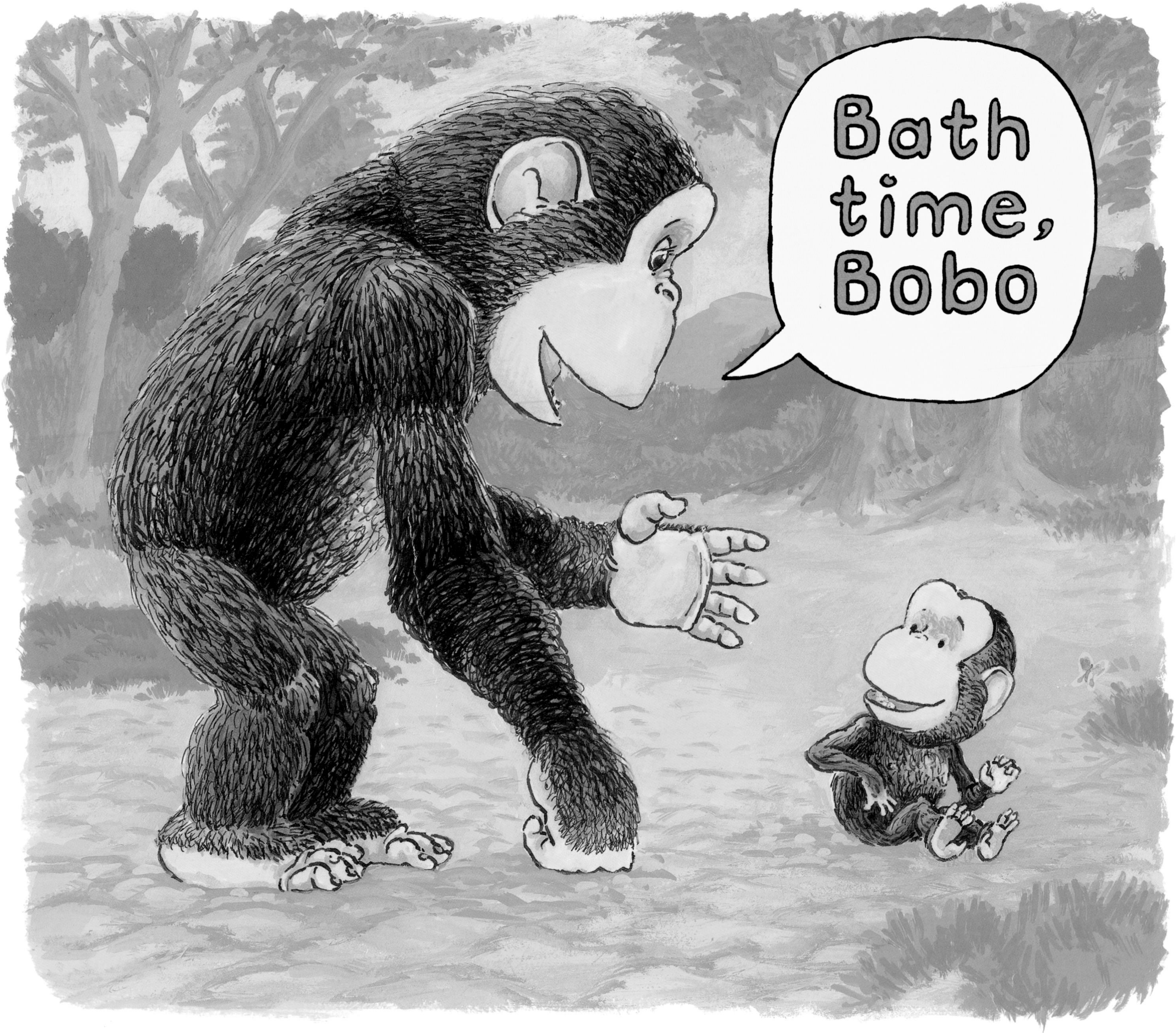
Bath time, Bobo

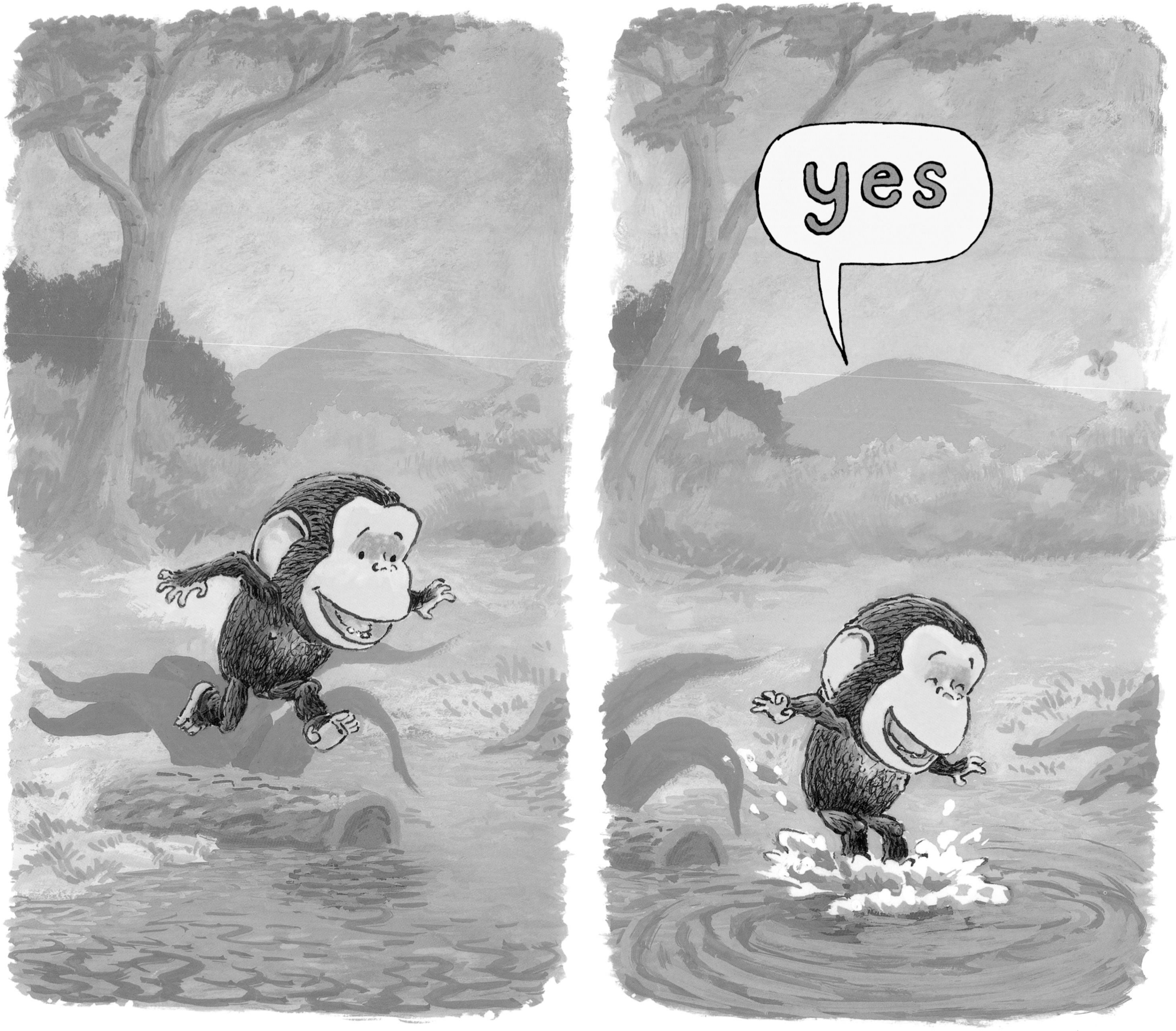
yes

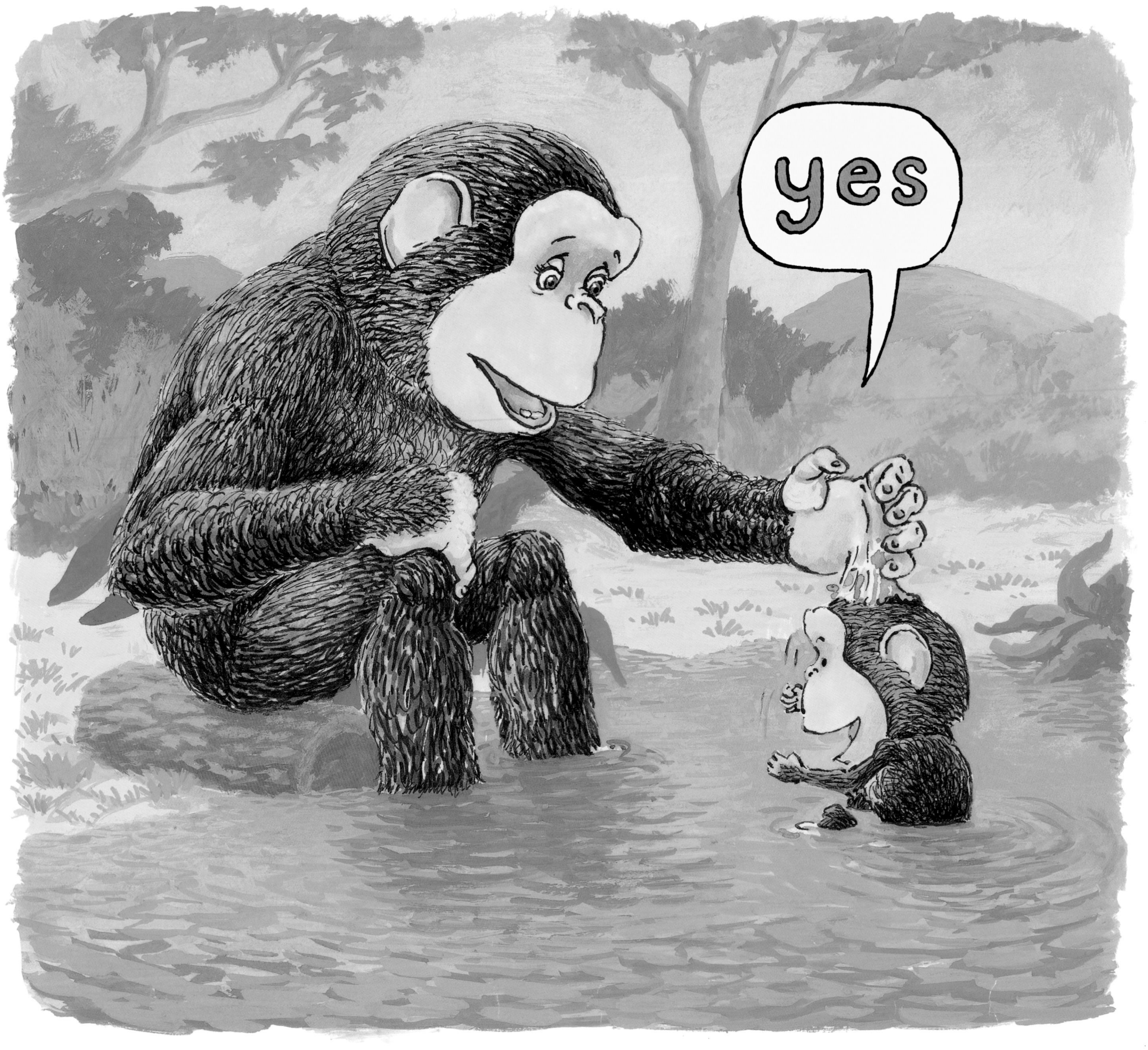
yes

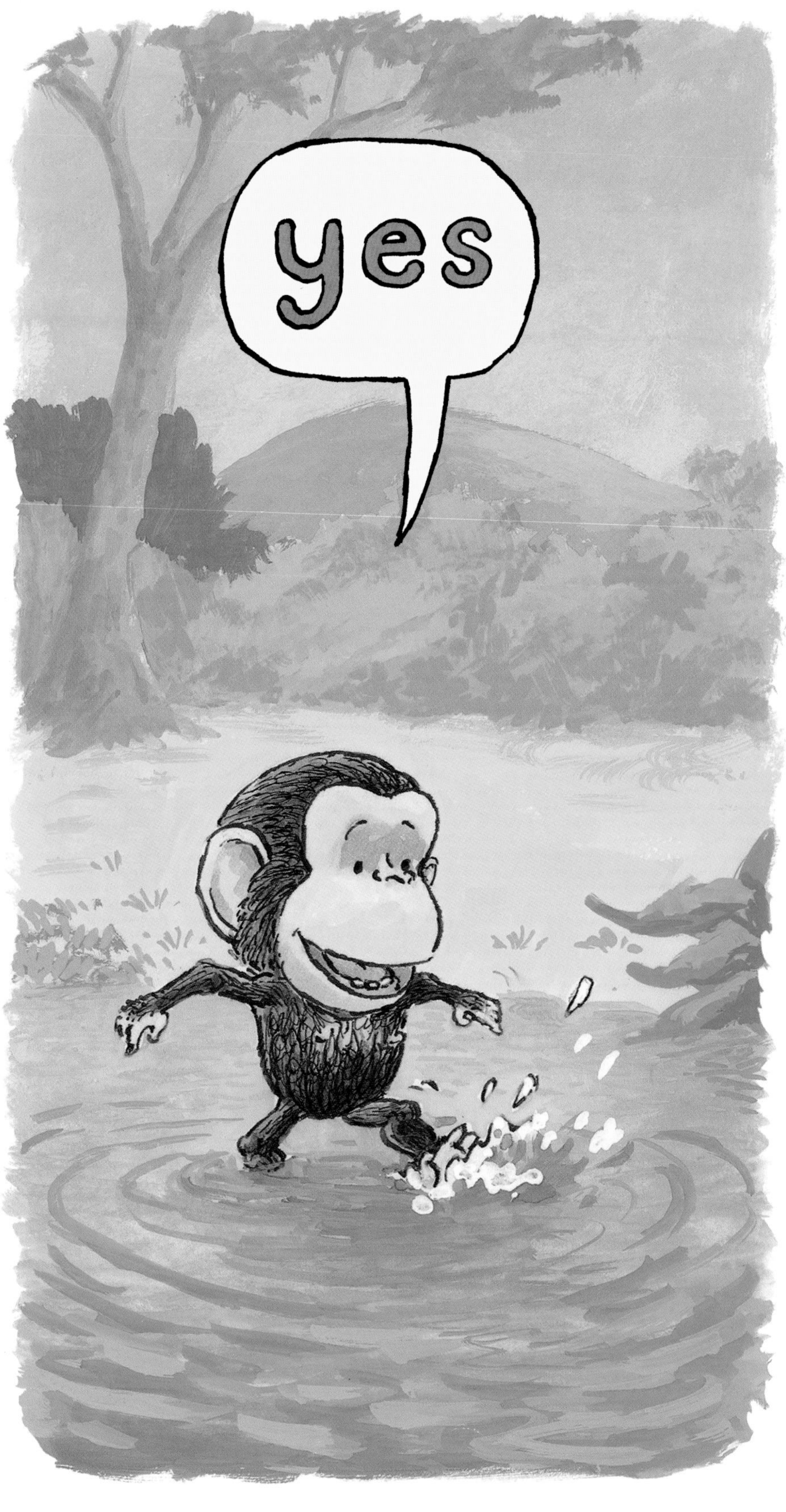
yes

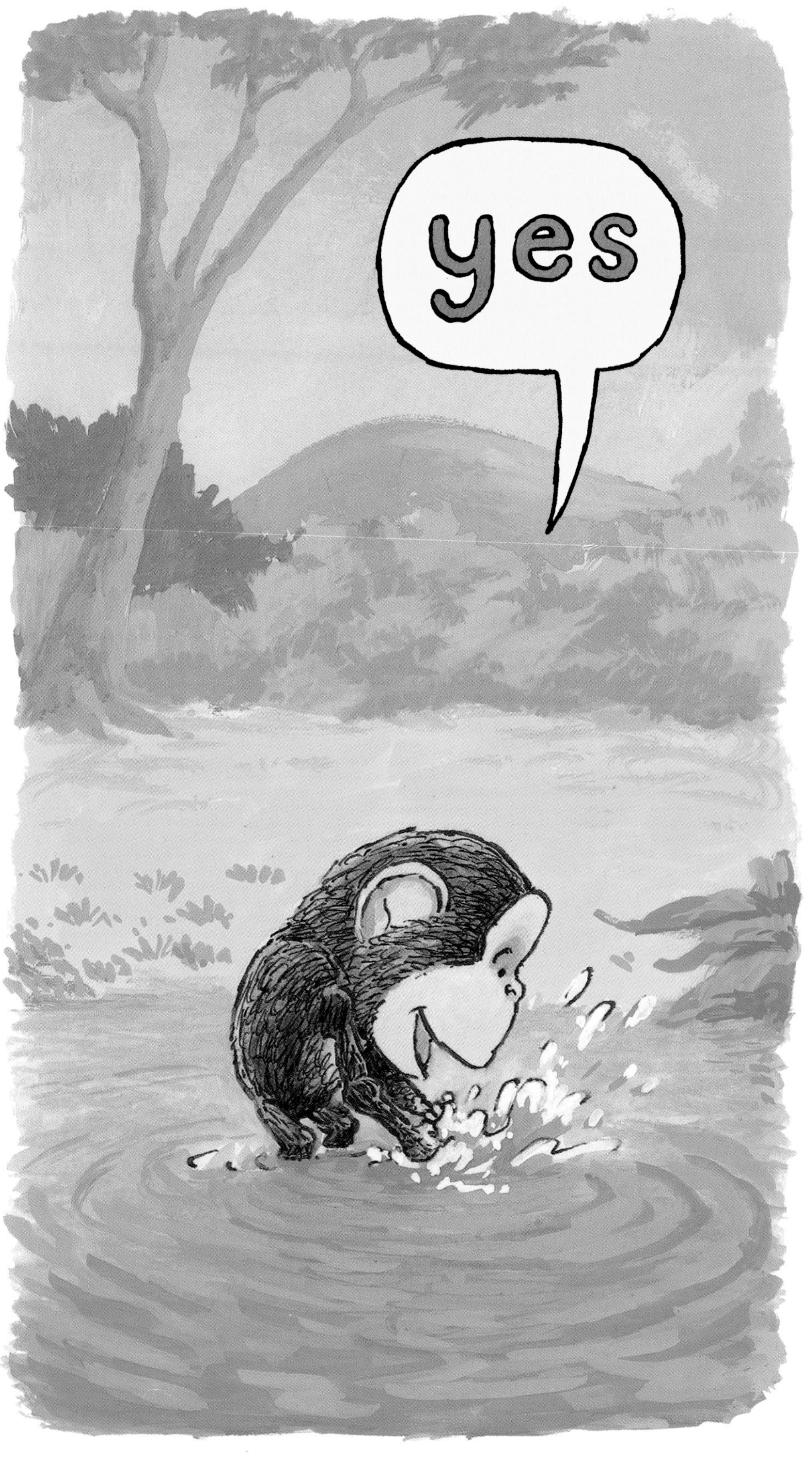
yes

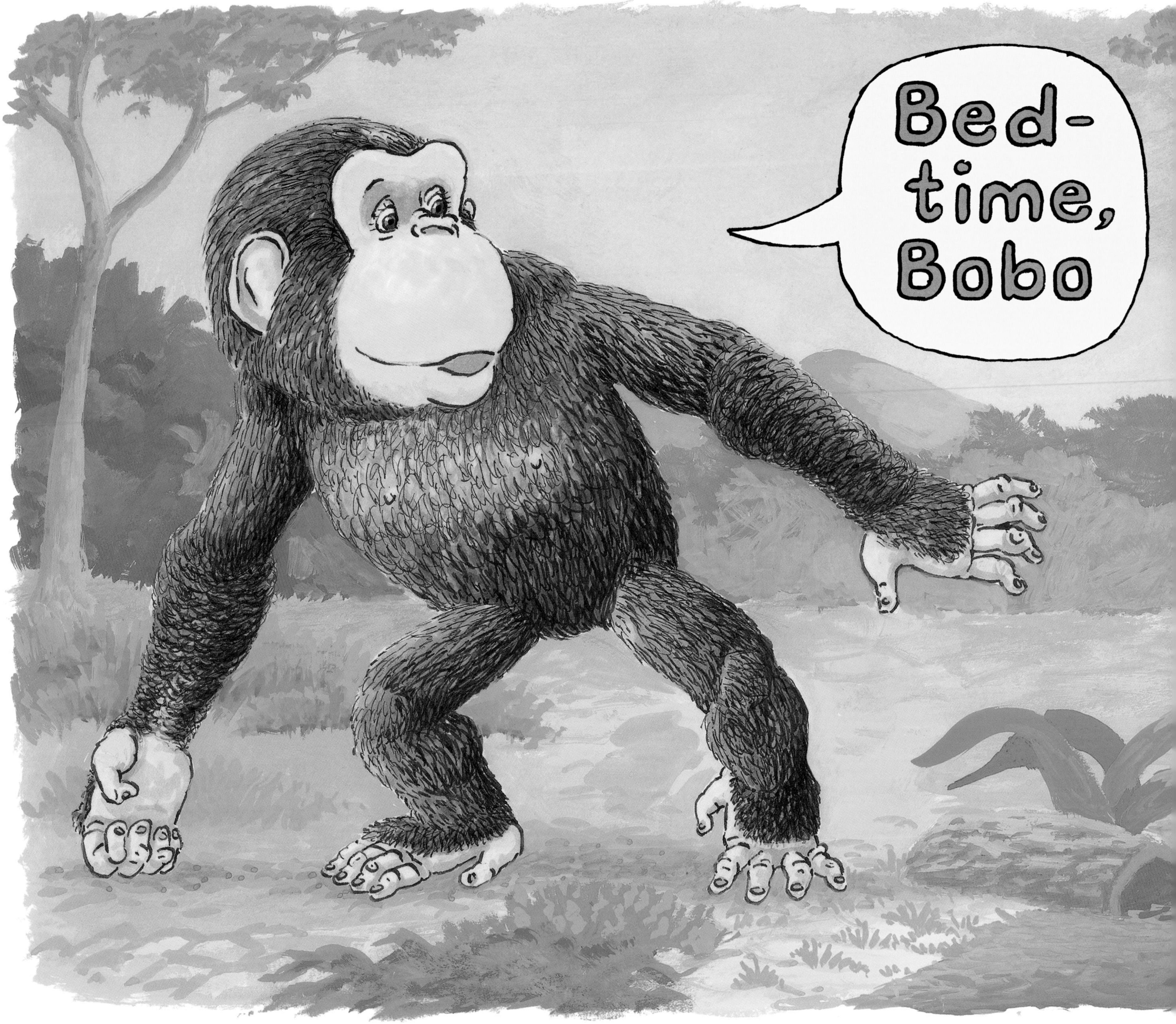
Bed-time, Bobo

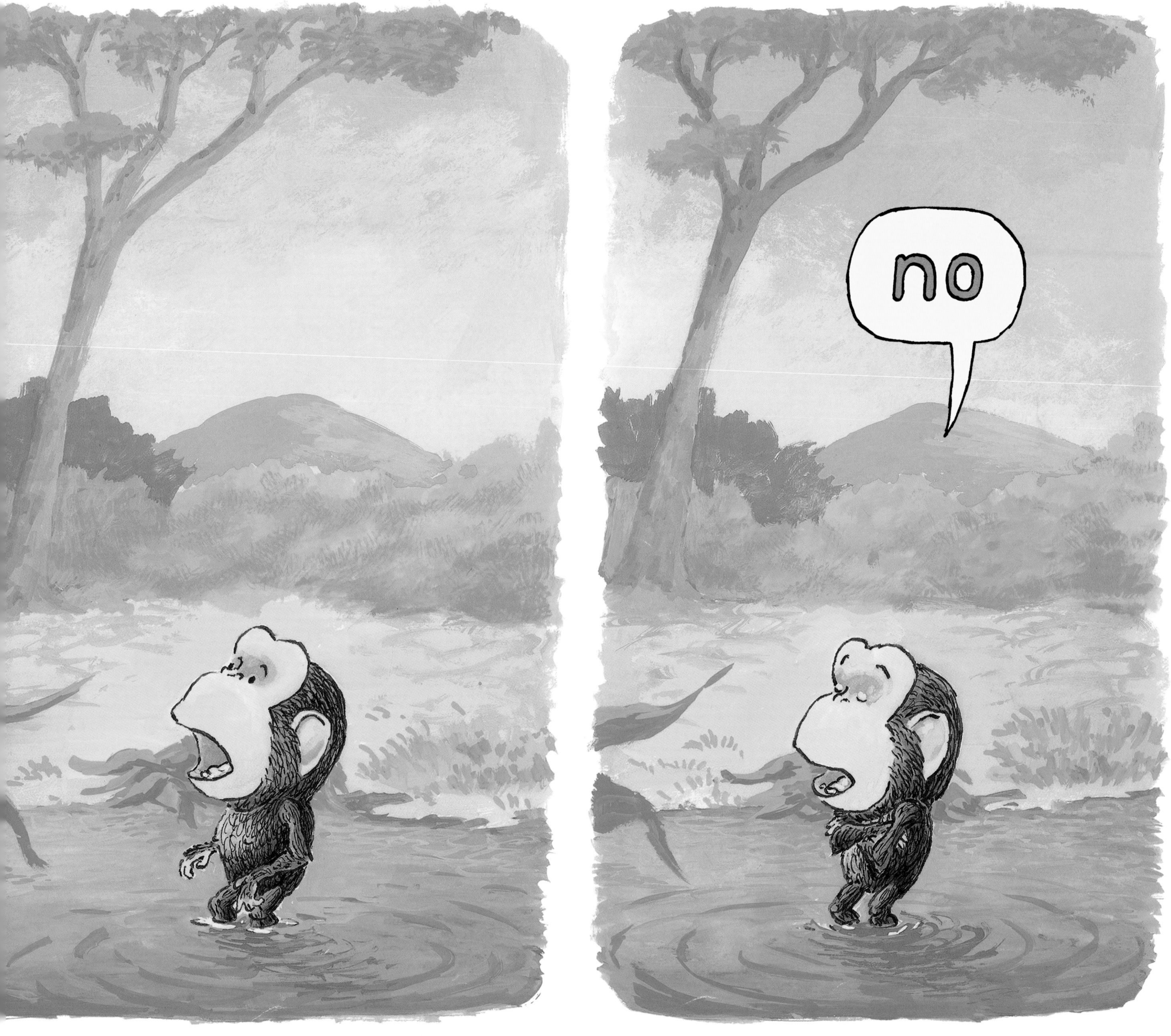
no

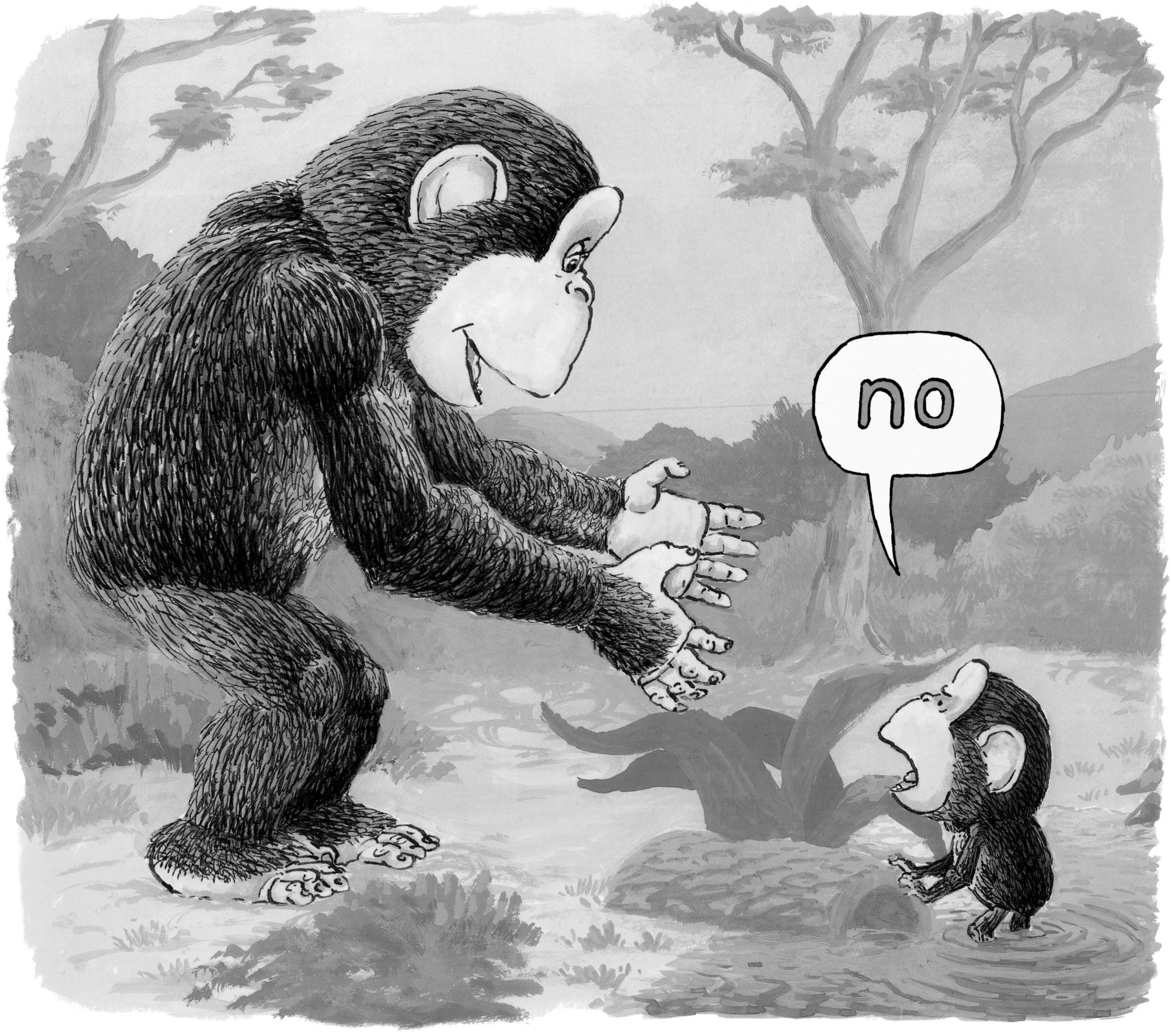
no

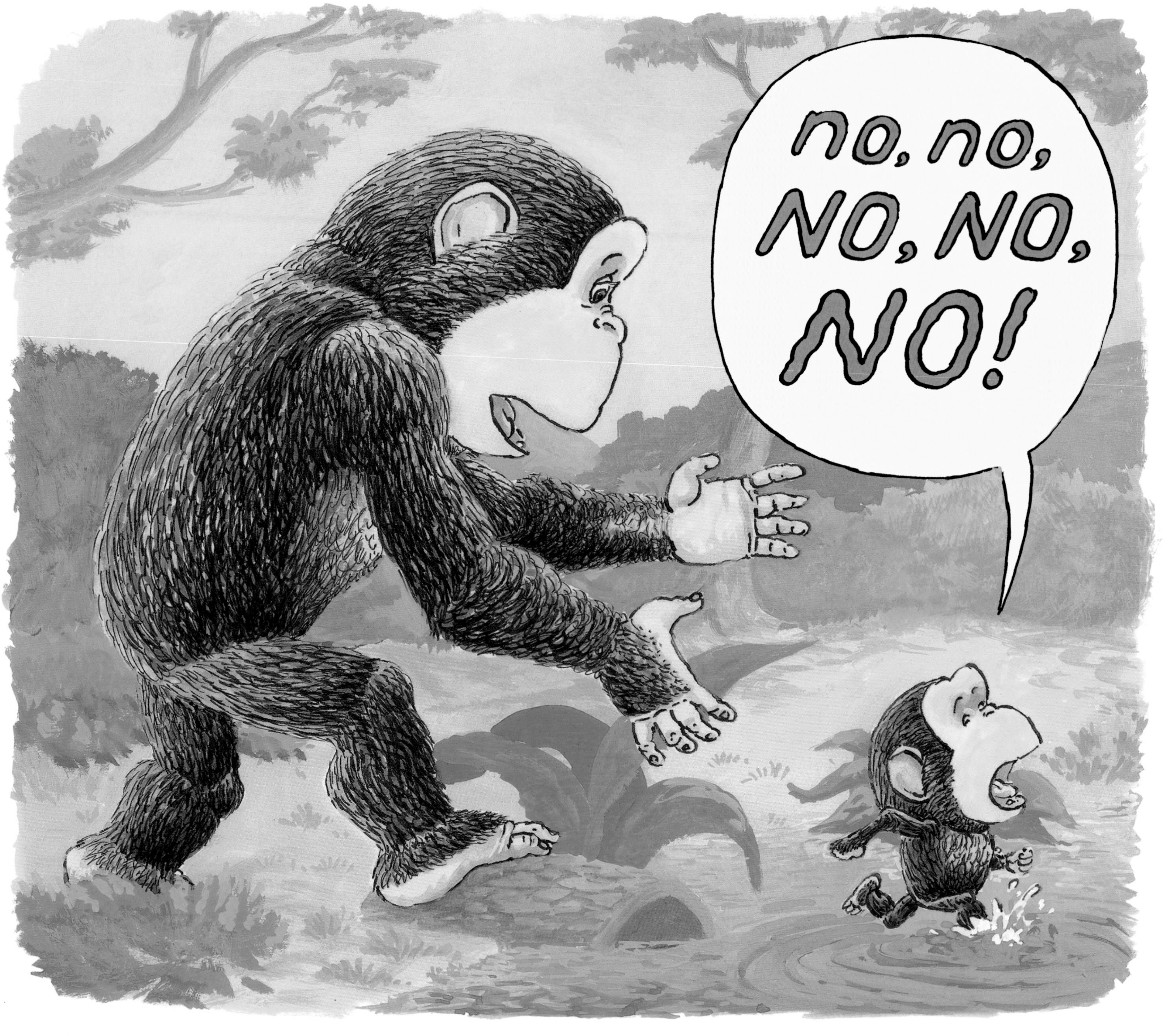
no, no,
NO, NO,
NO!

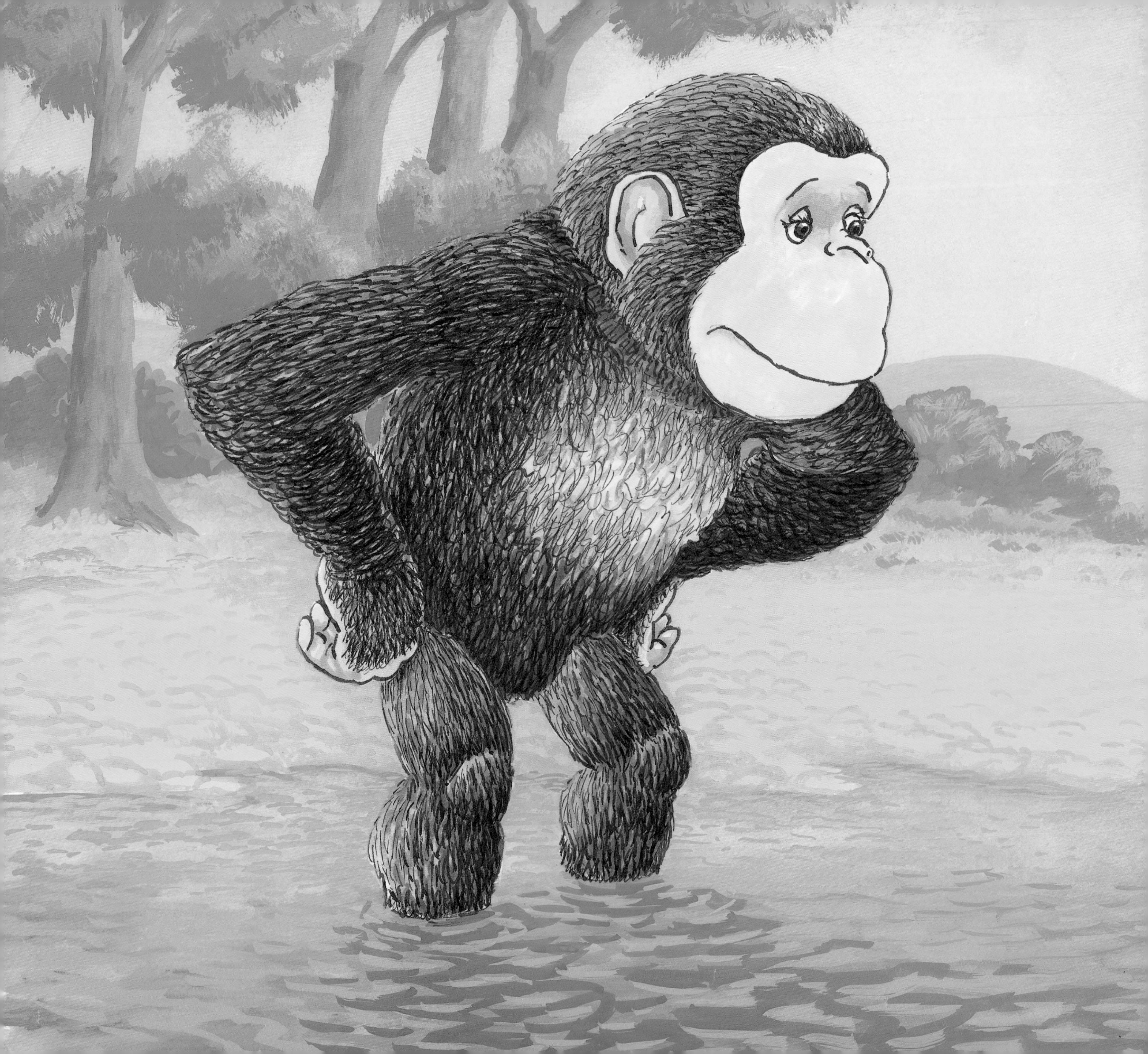

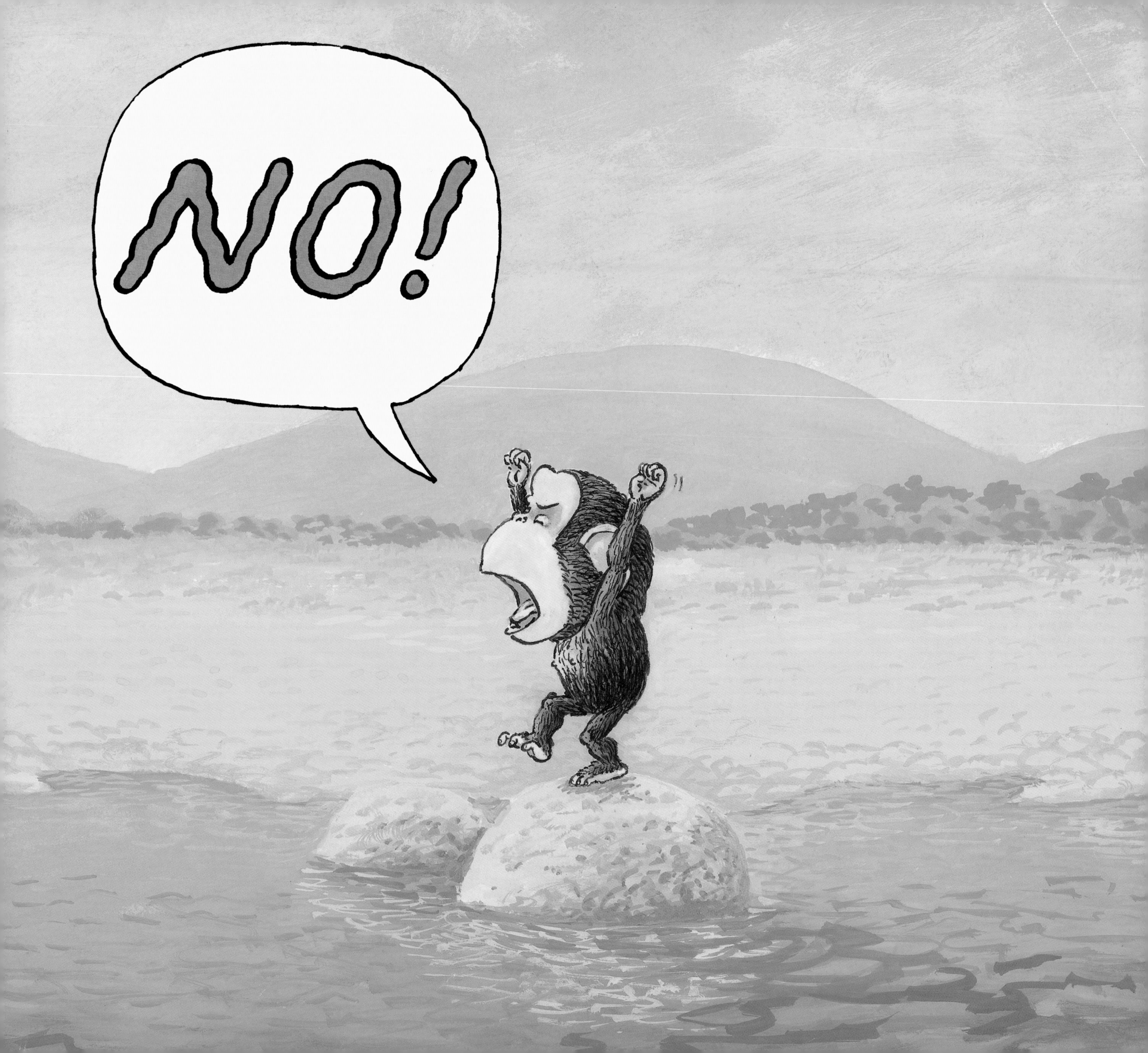
NO!

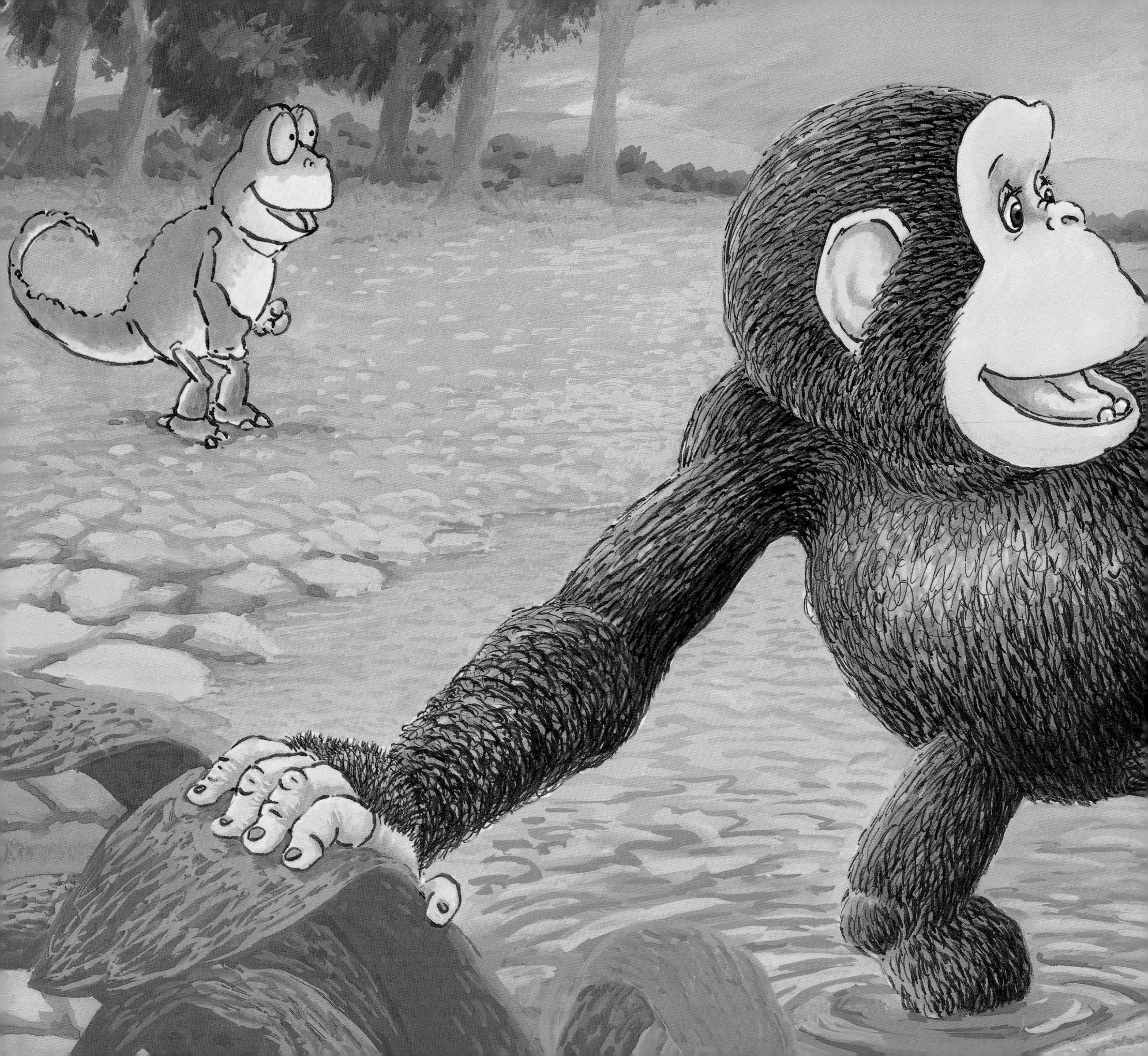

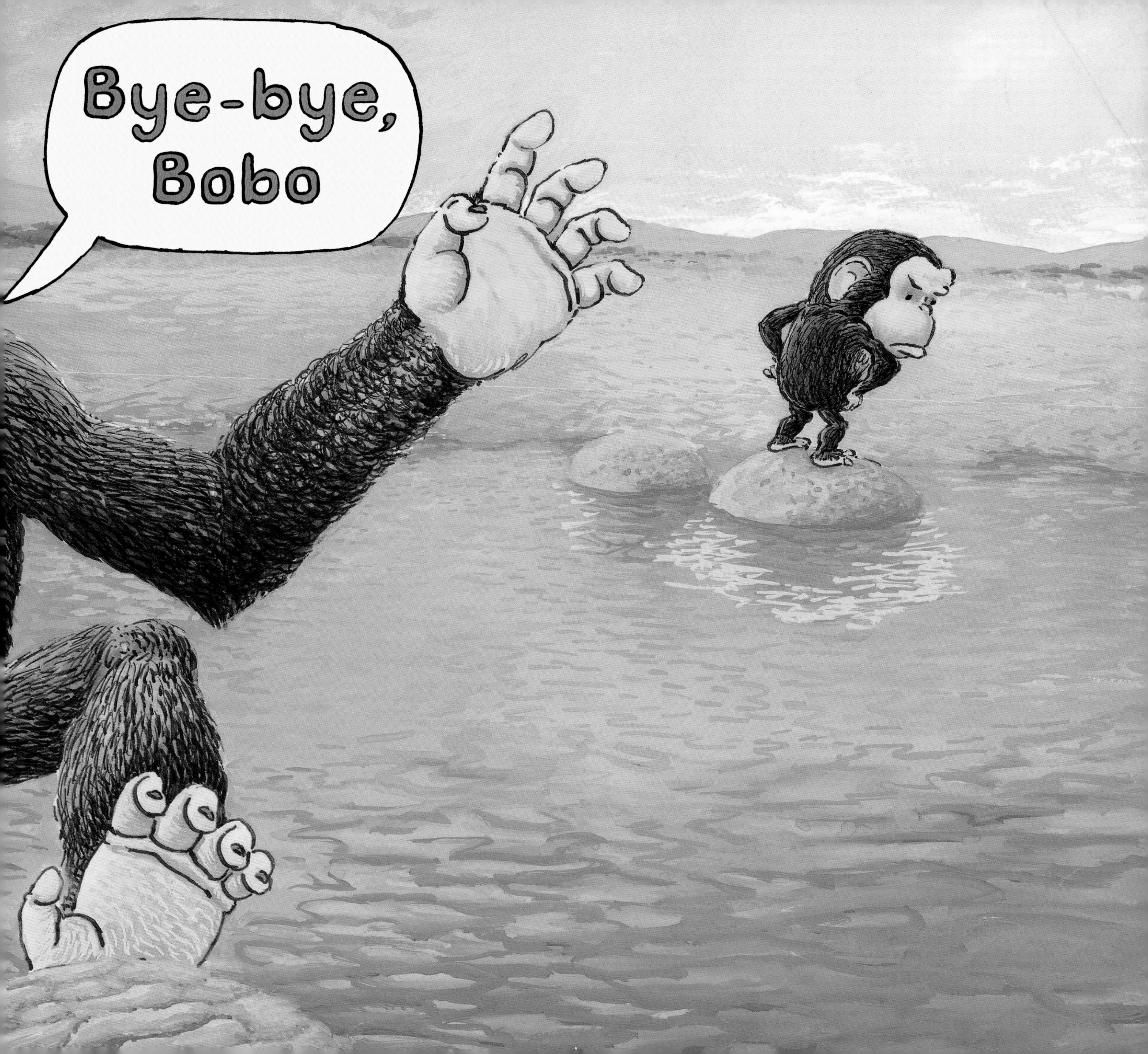
Bye-bye, Bobo

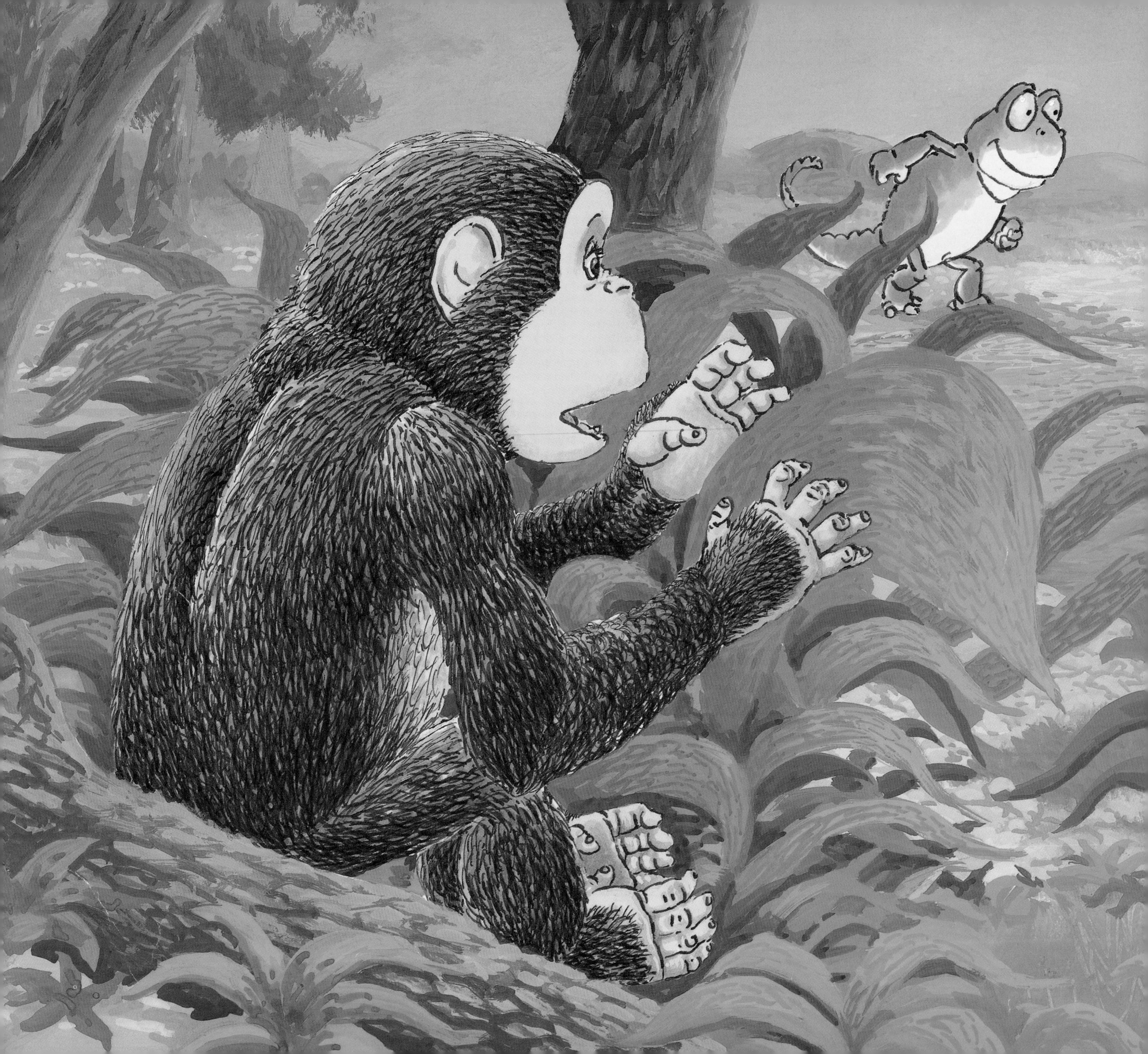

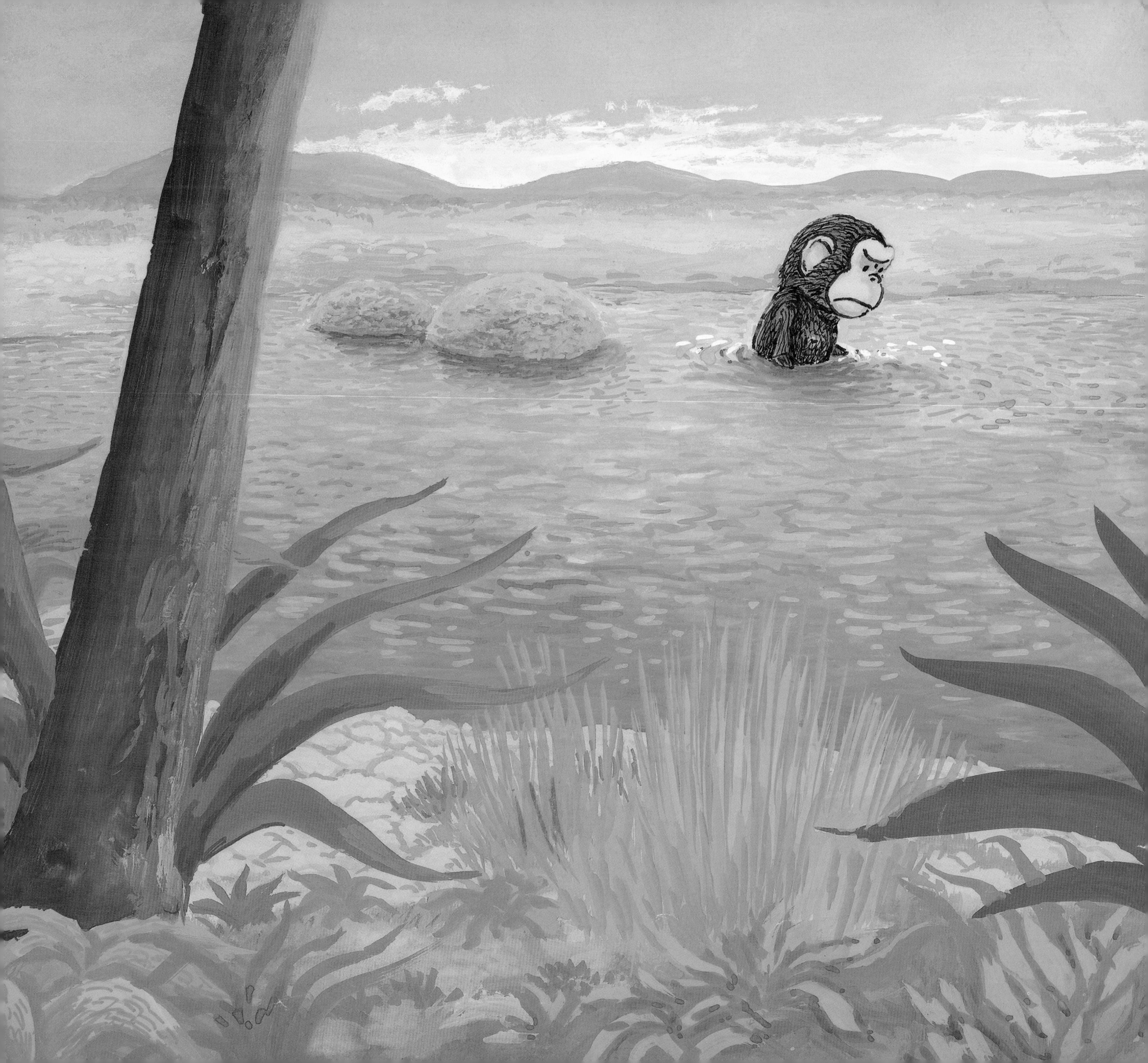

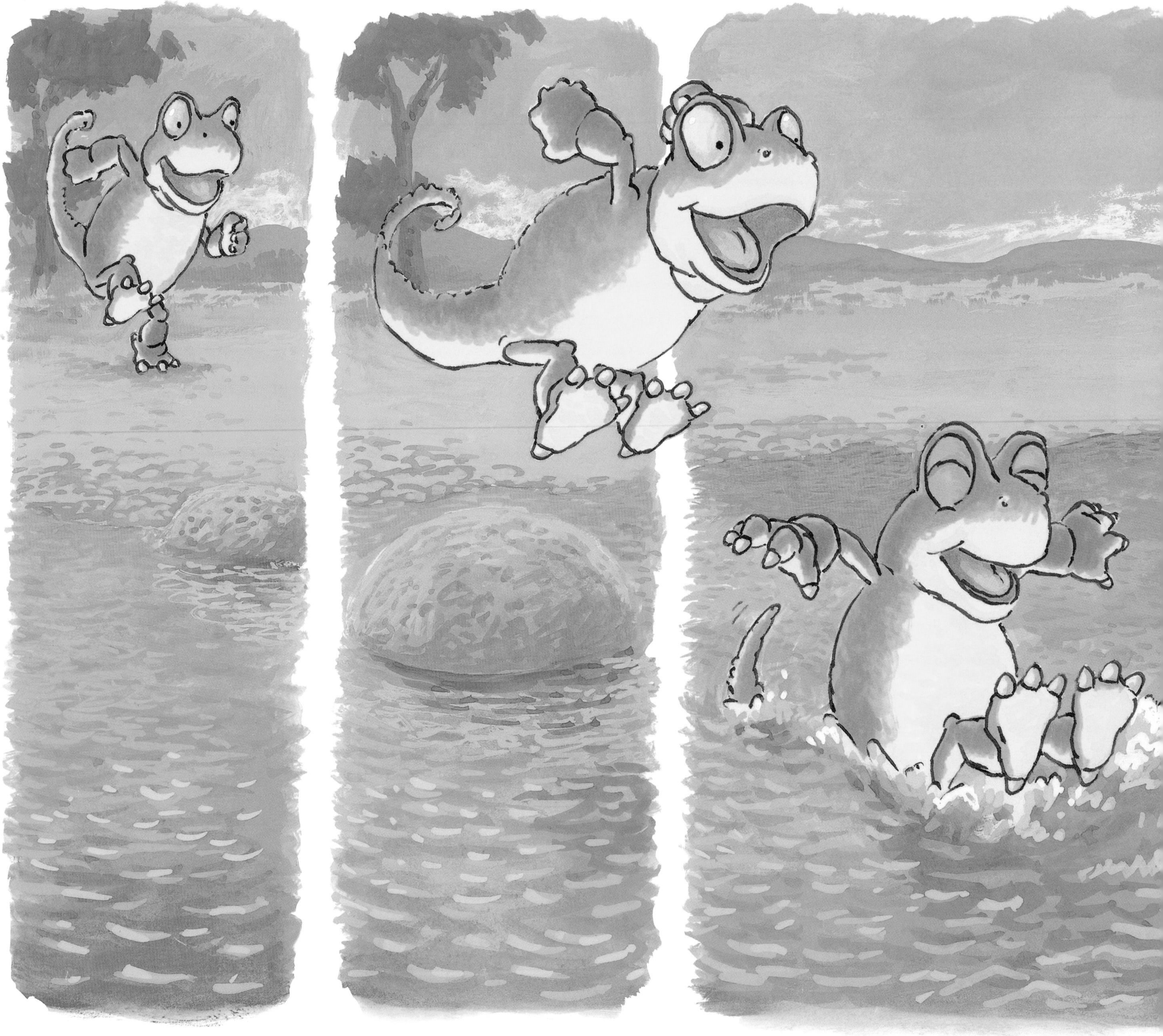

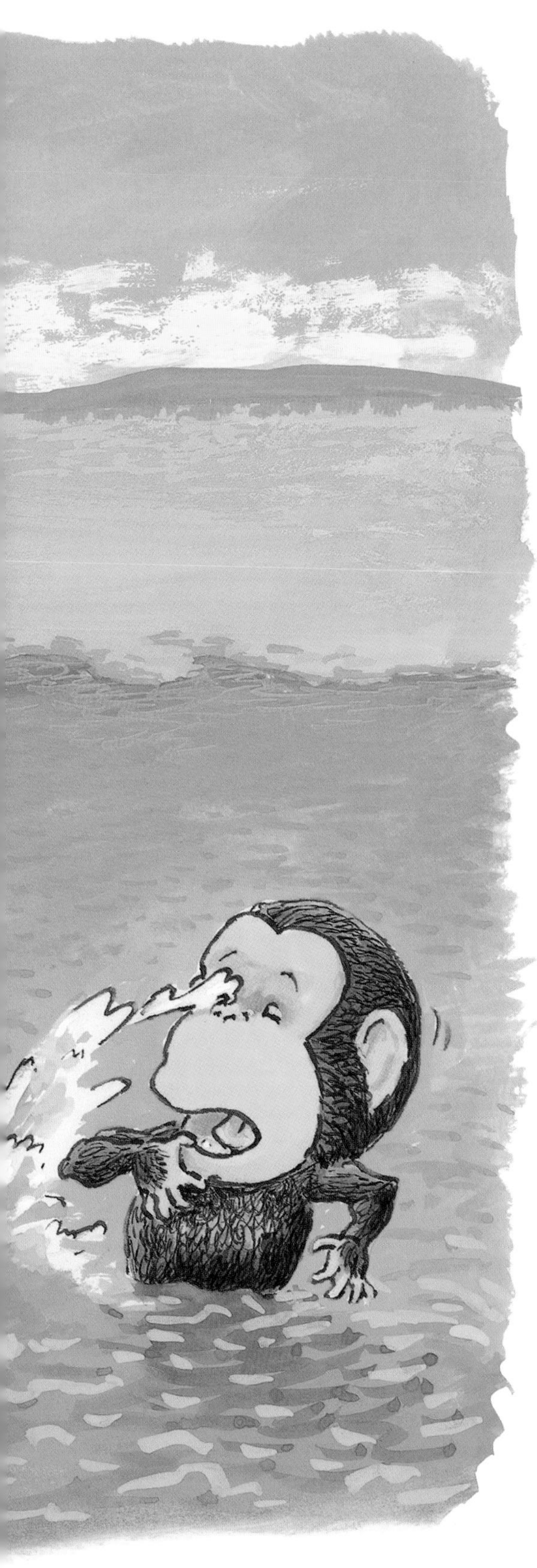

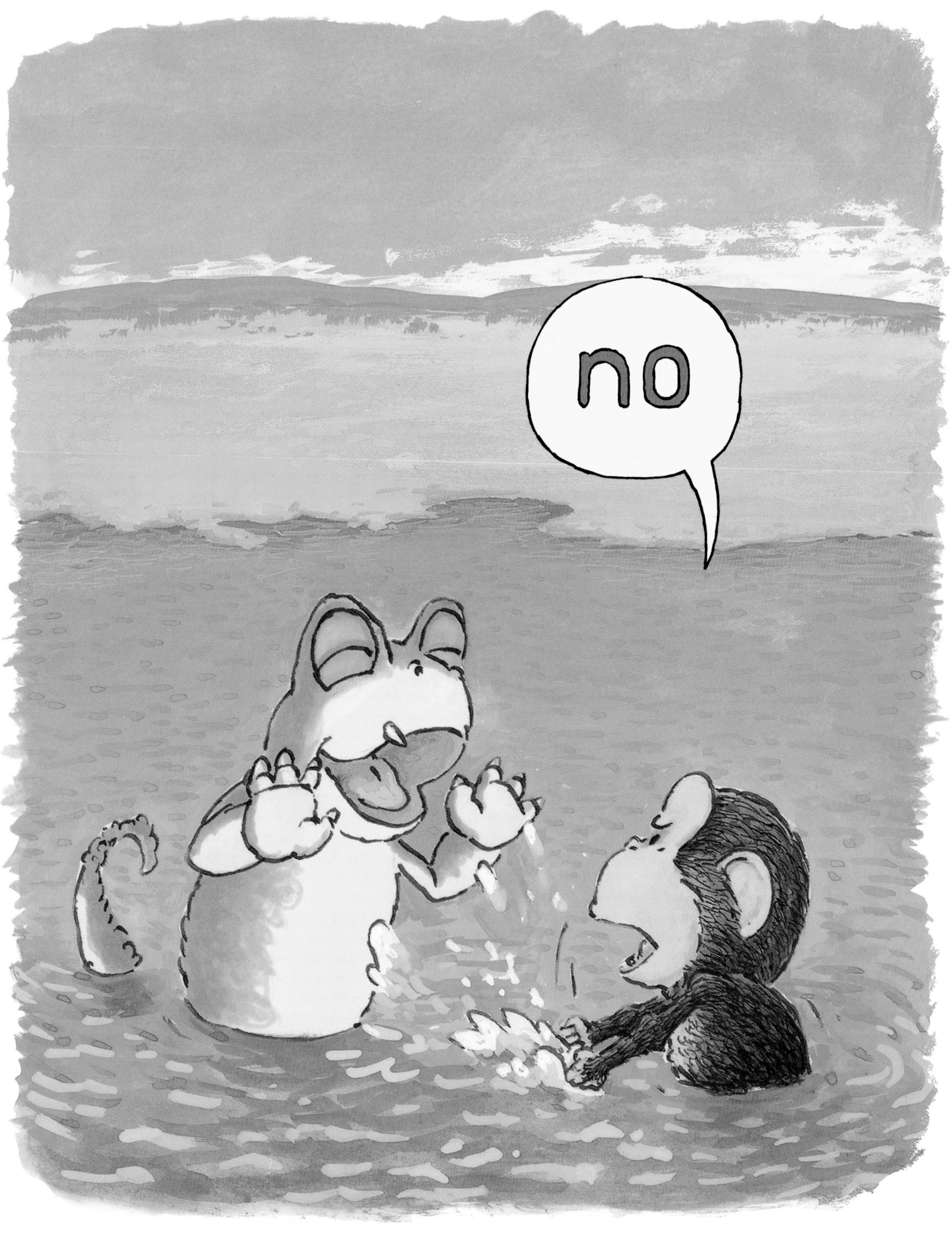
no

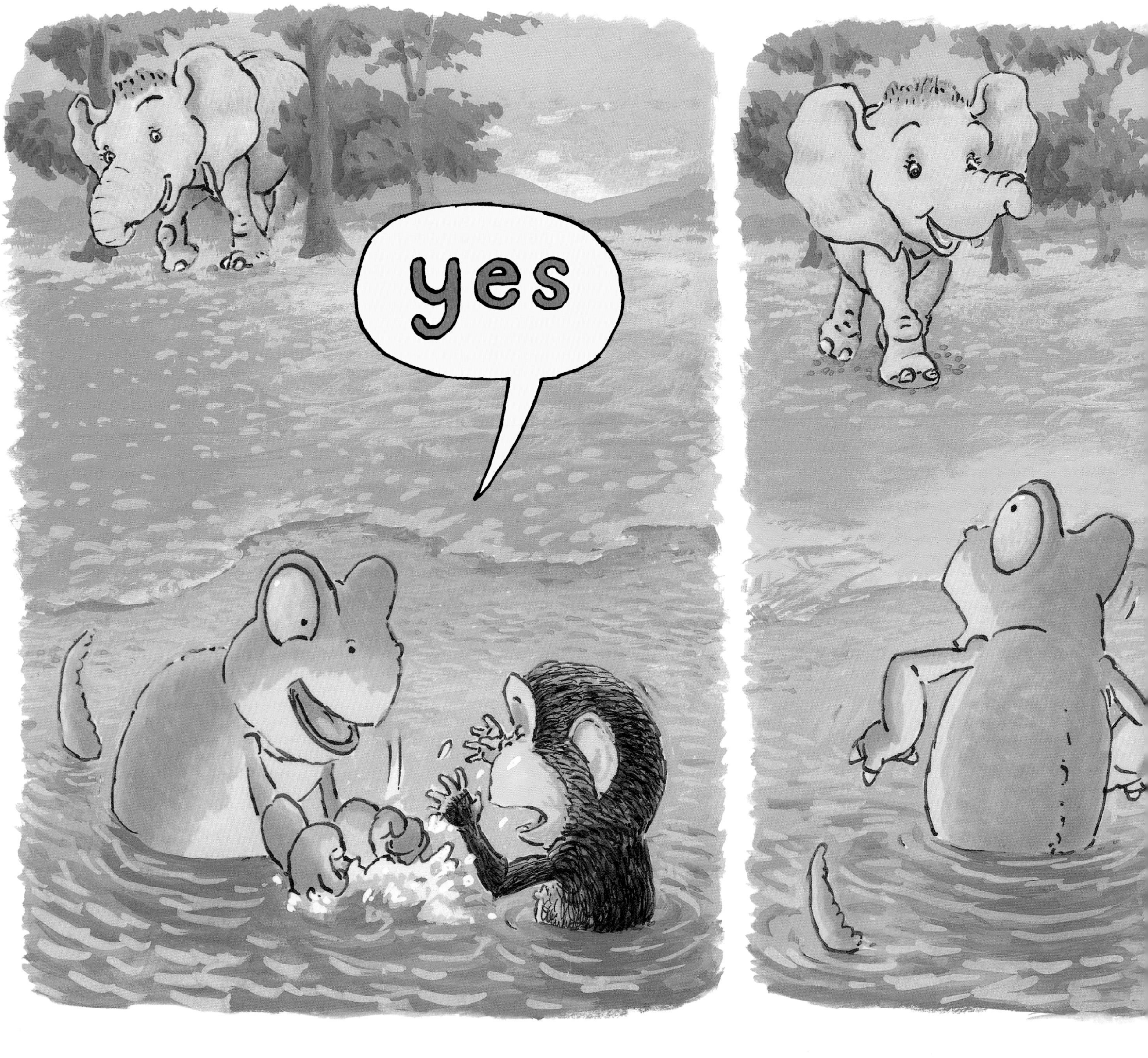
yes

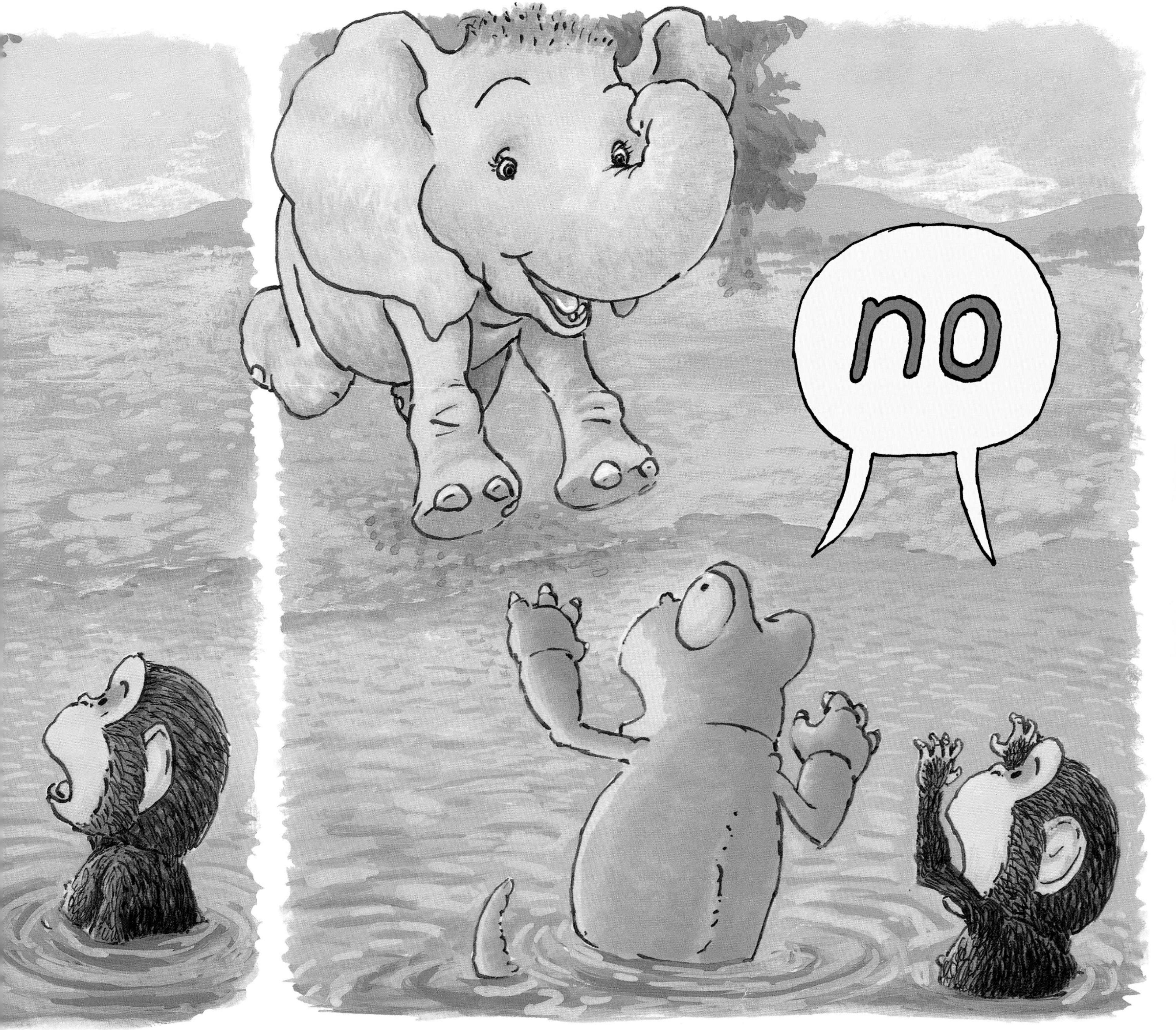
no

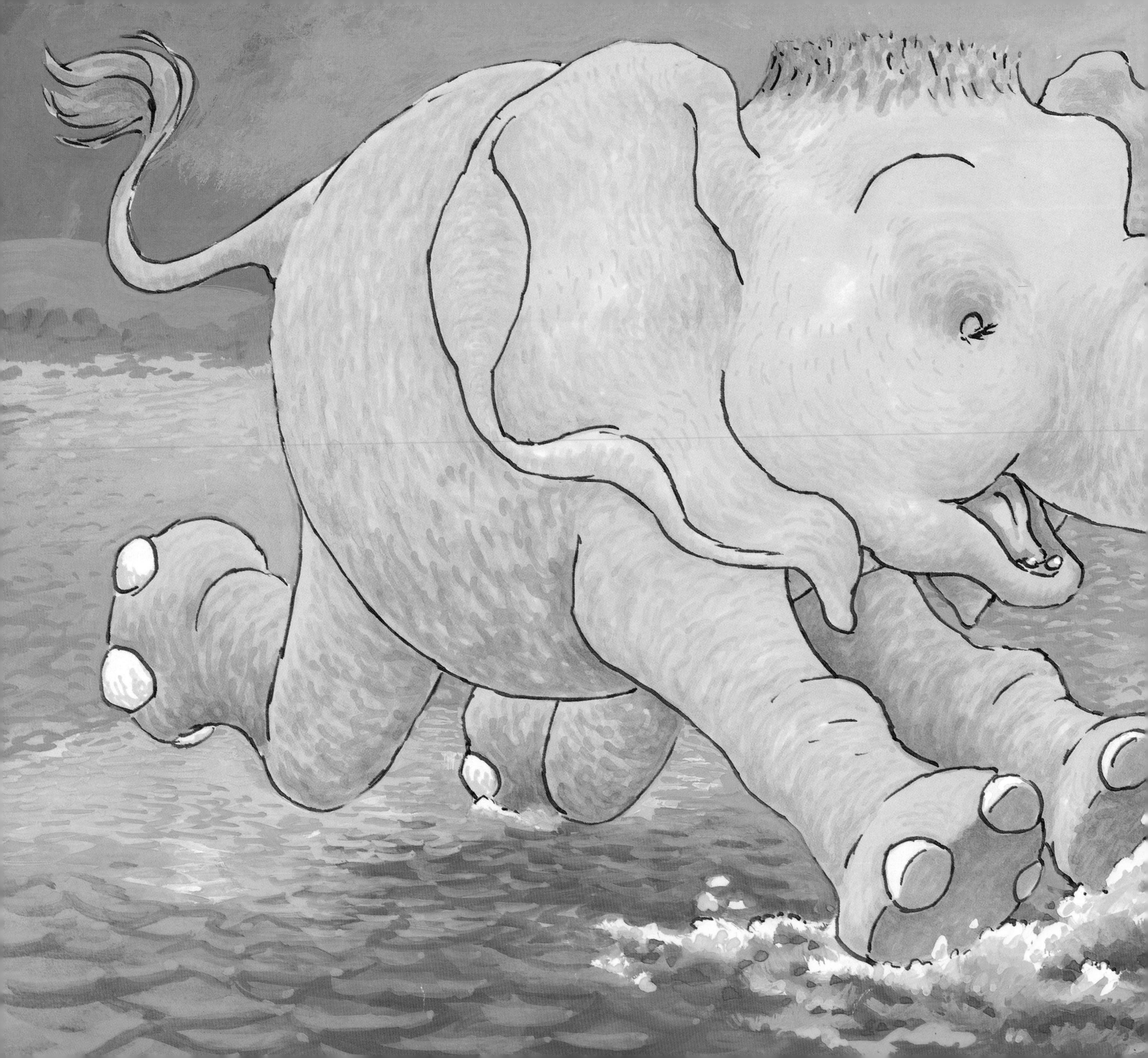

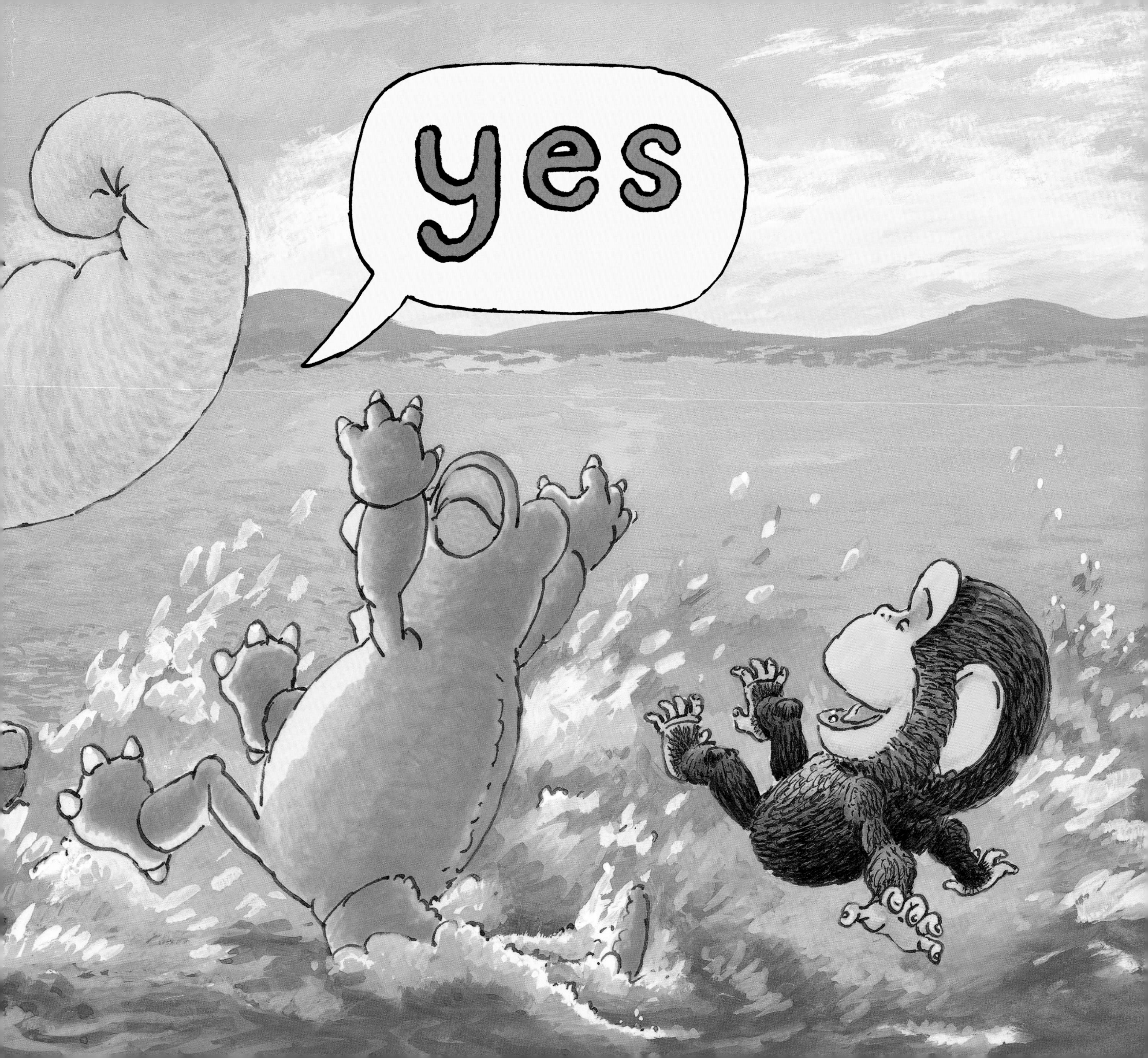
yes

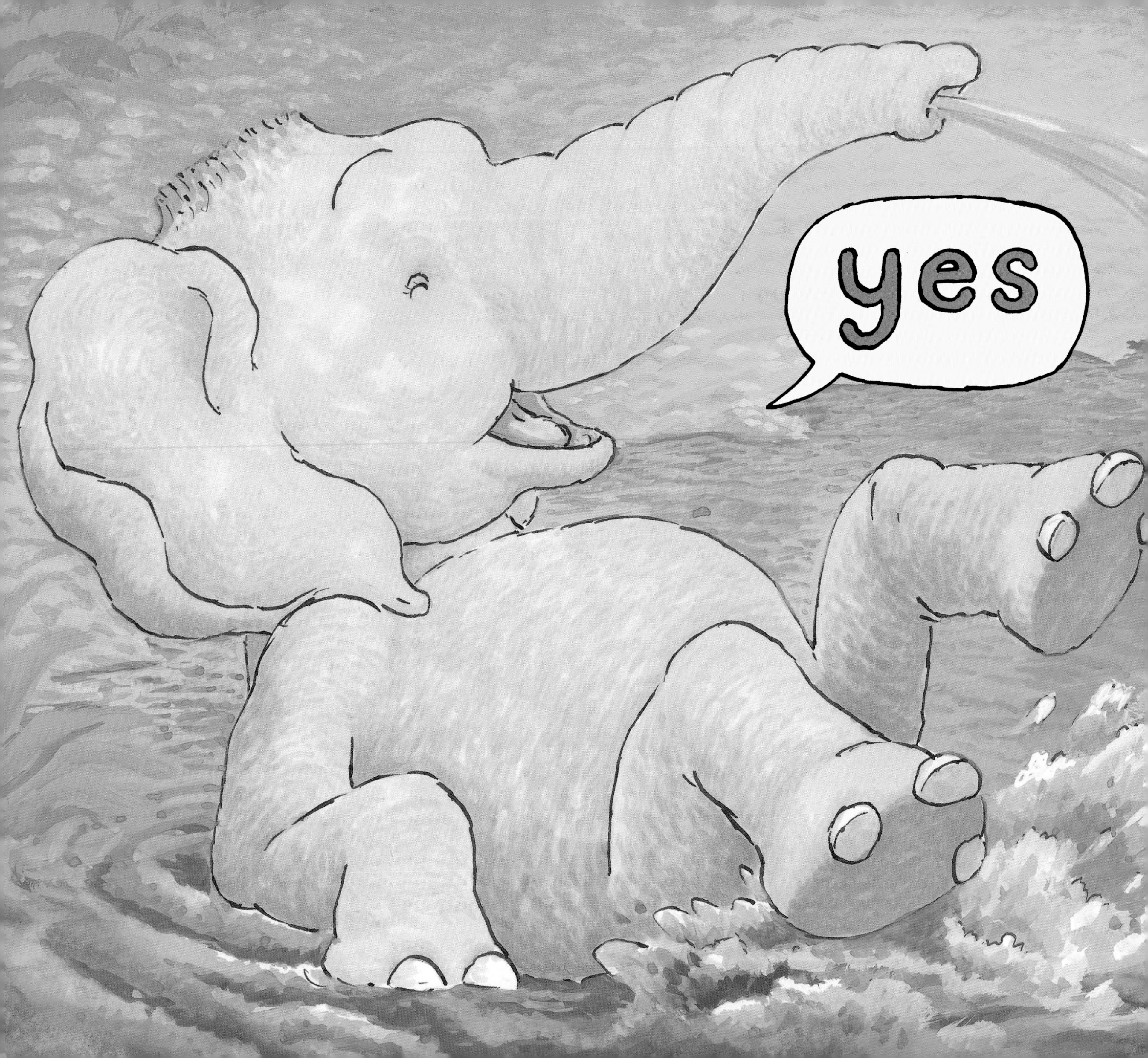
yes

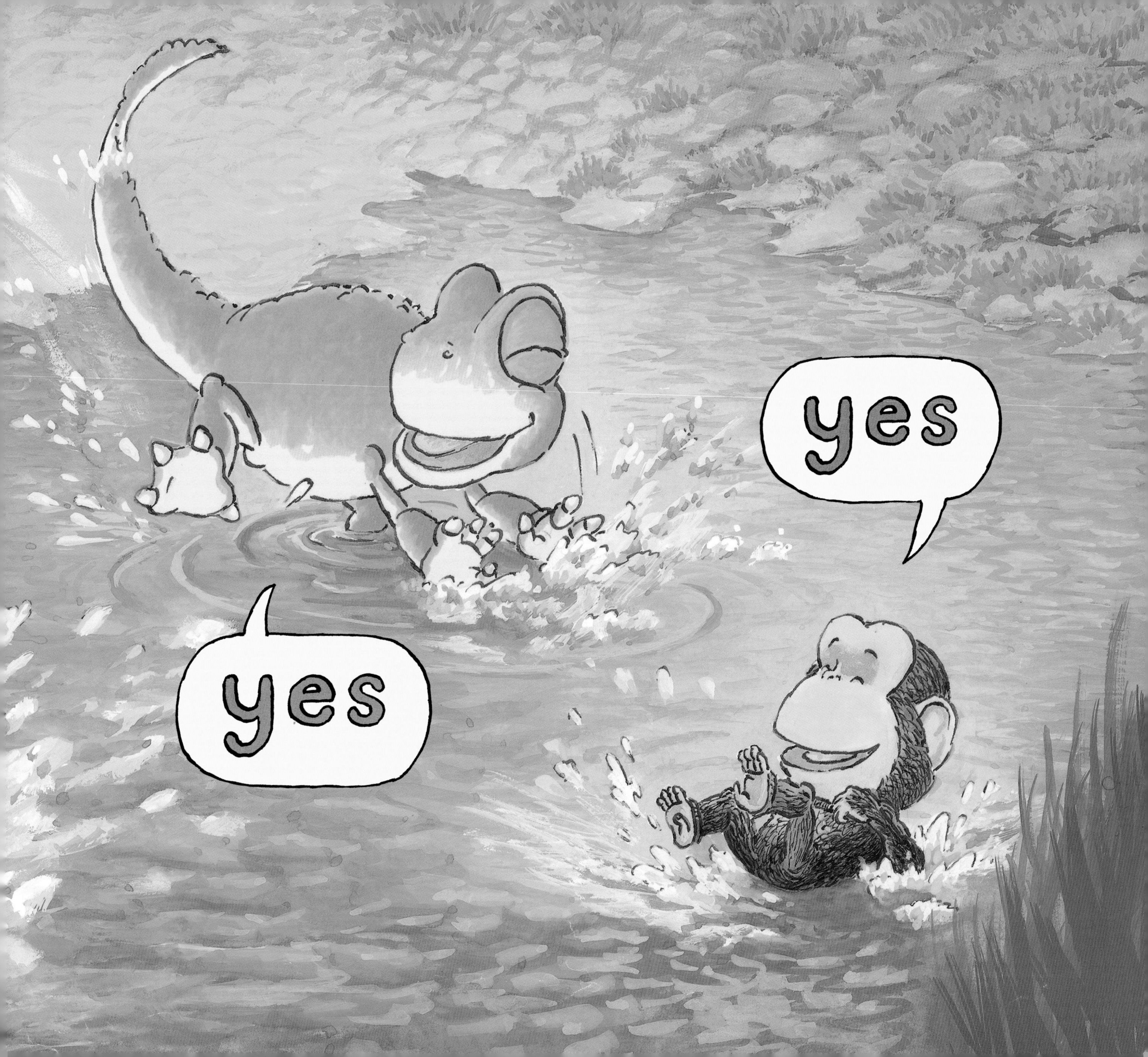
yes
yes

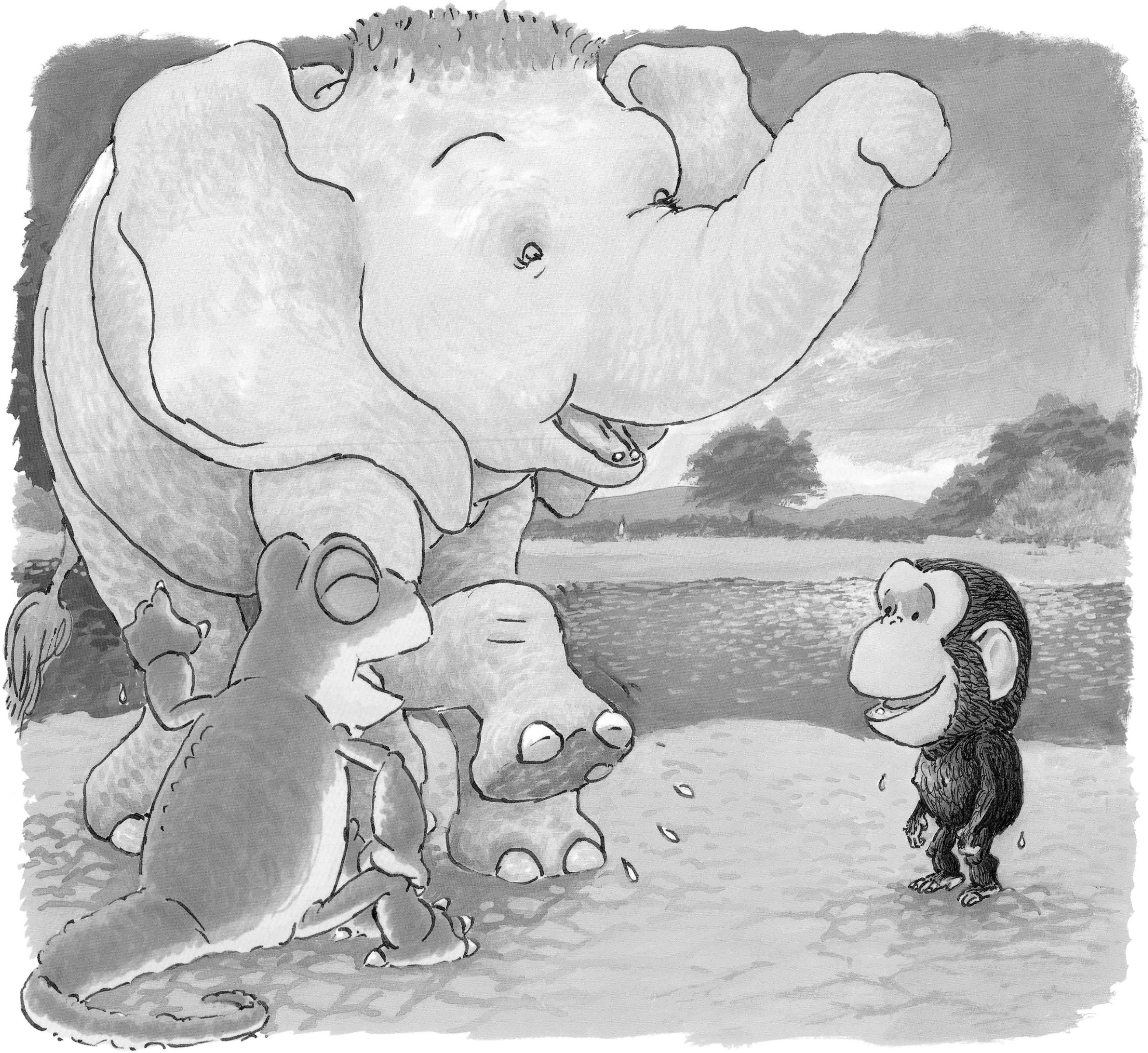

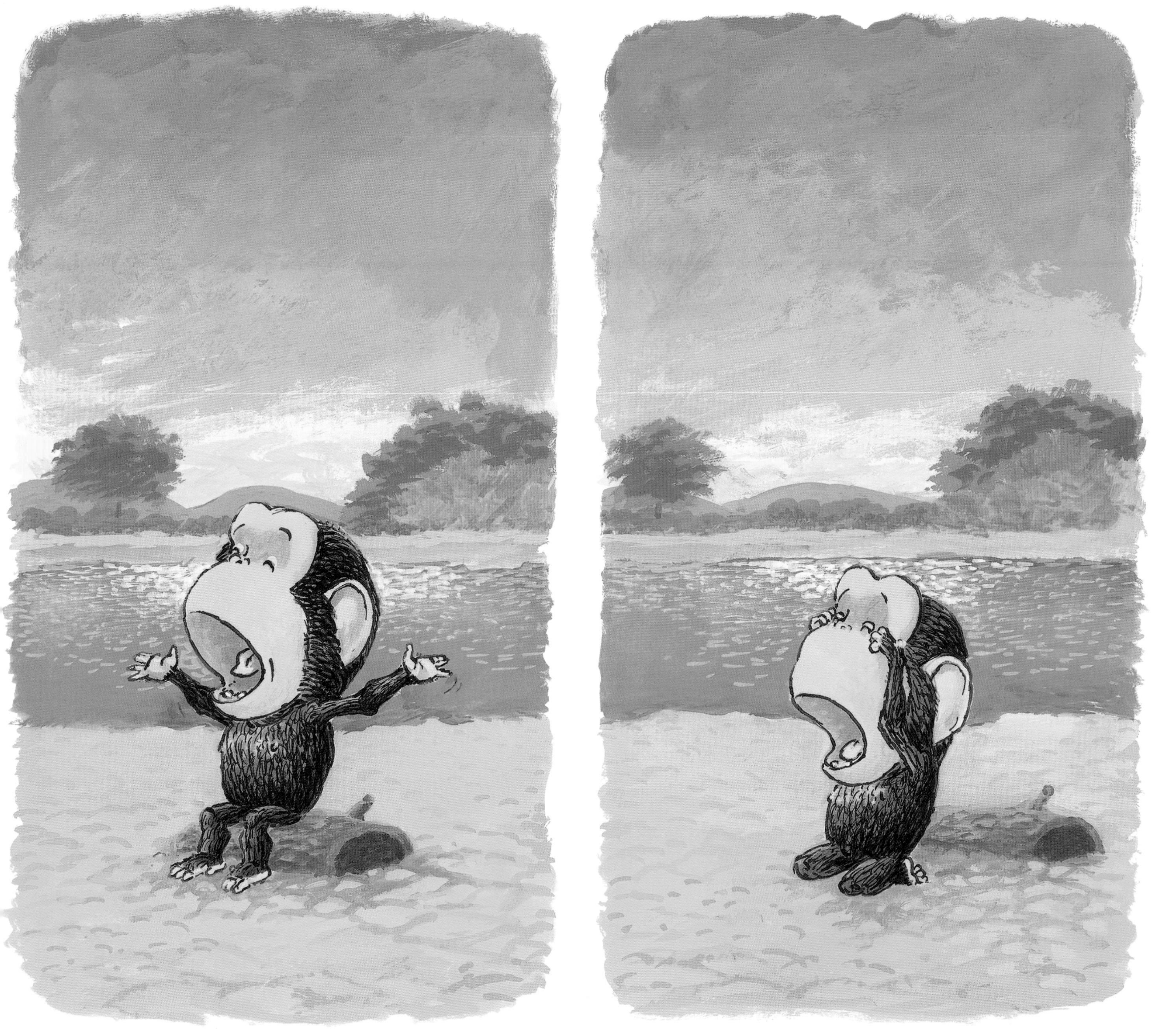

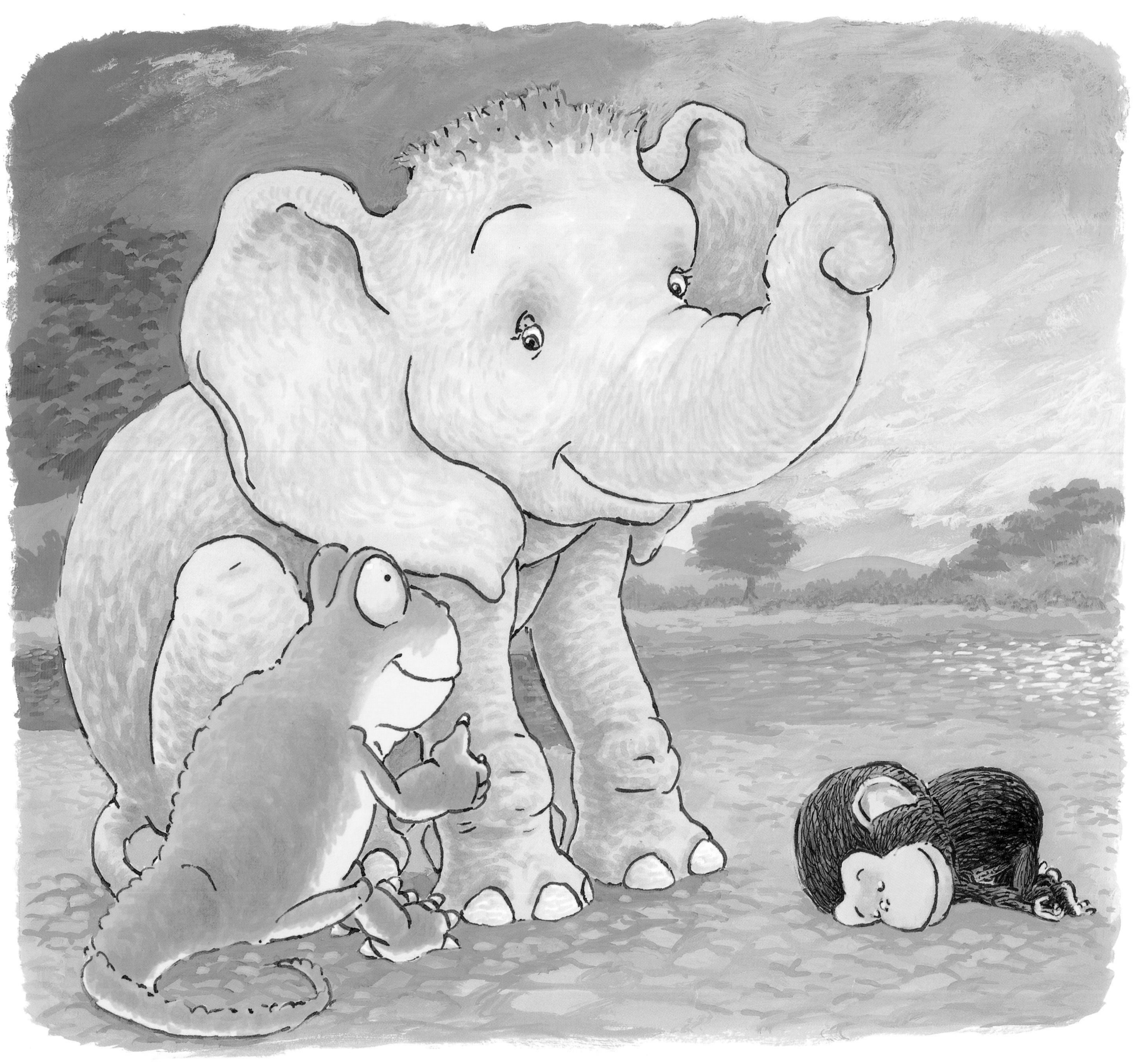

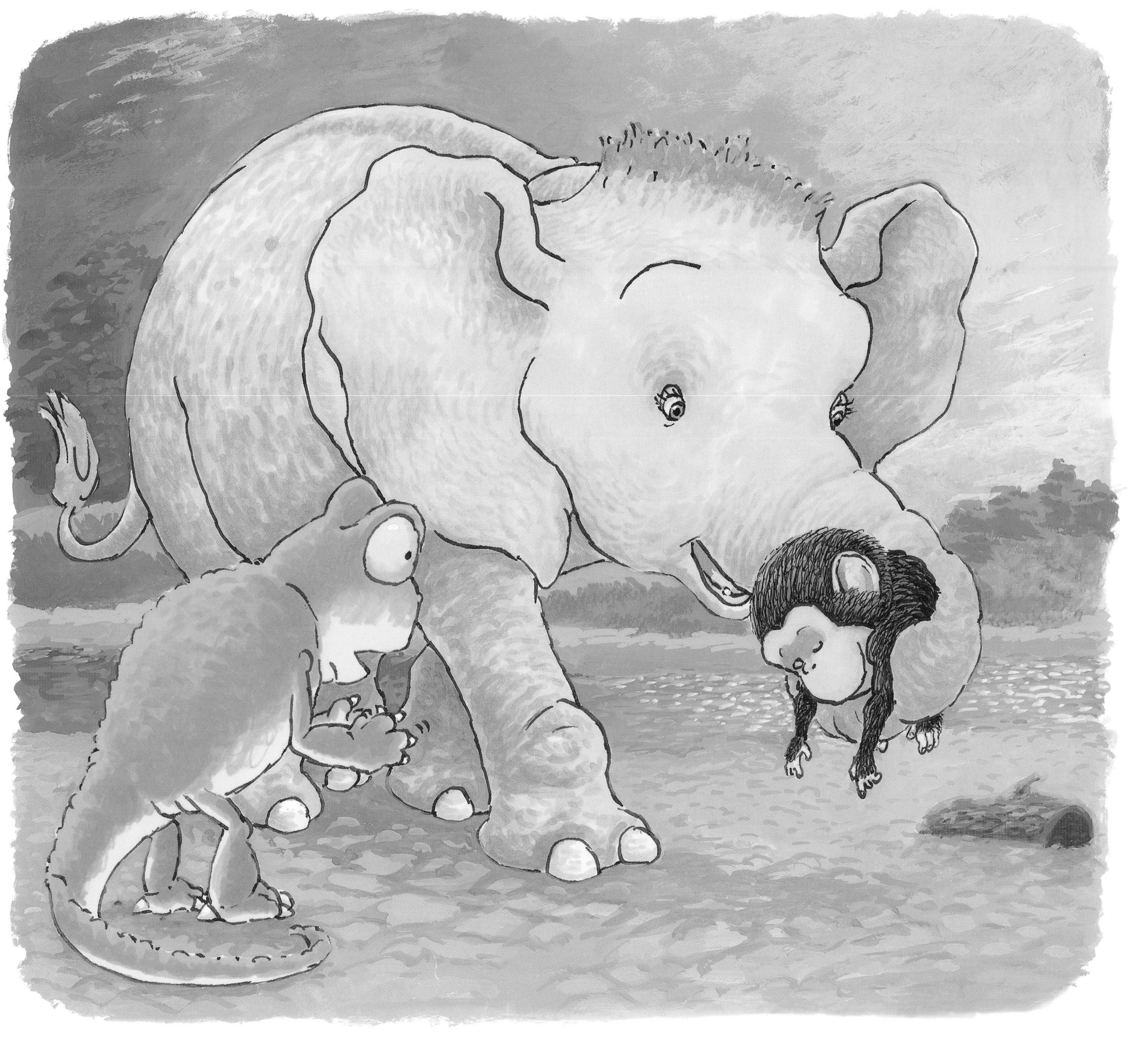

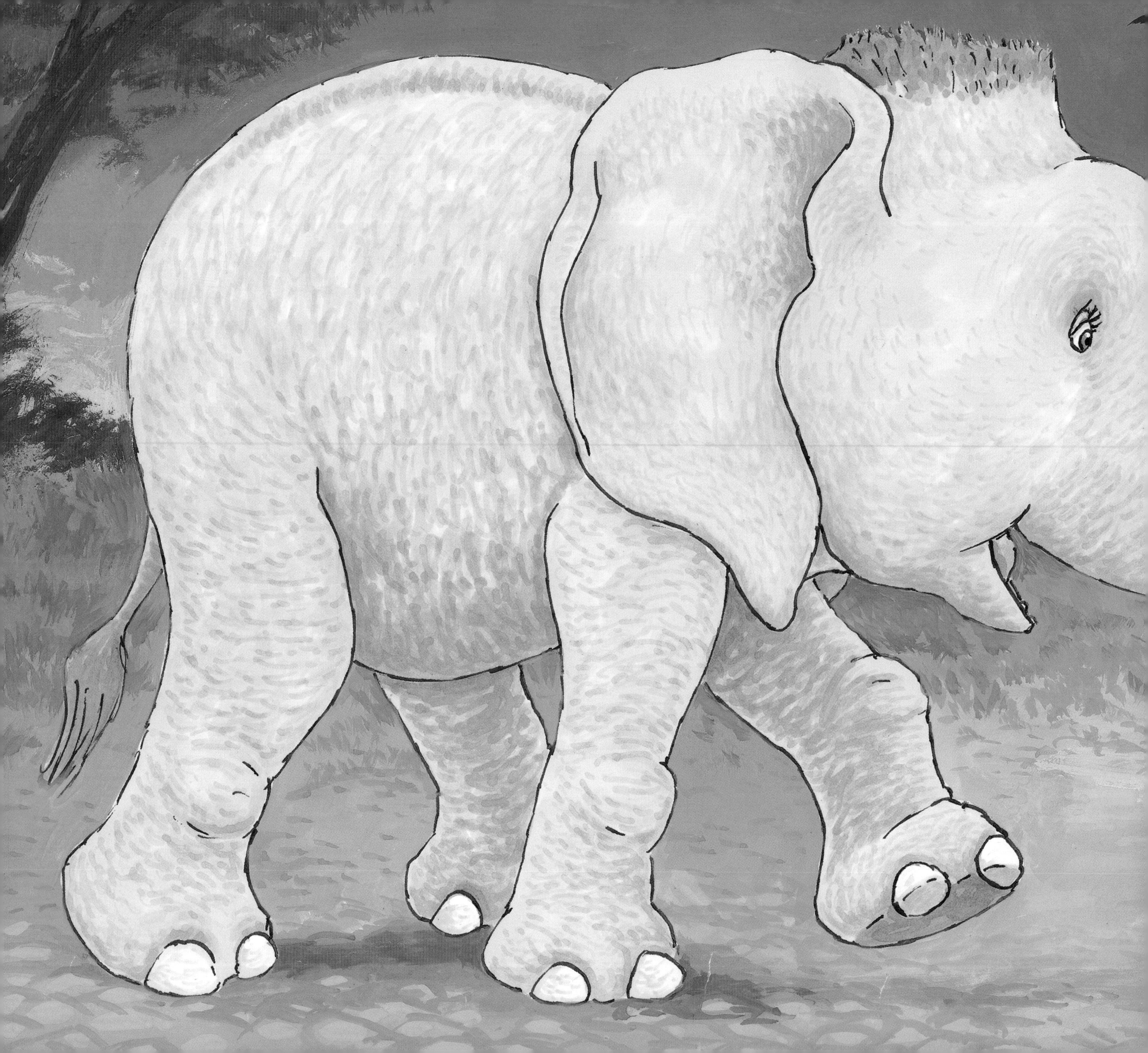

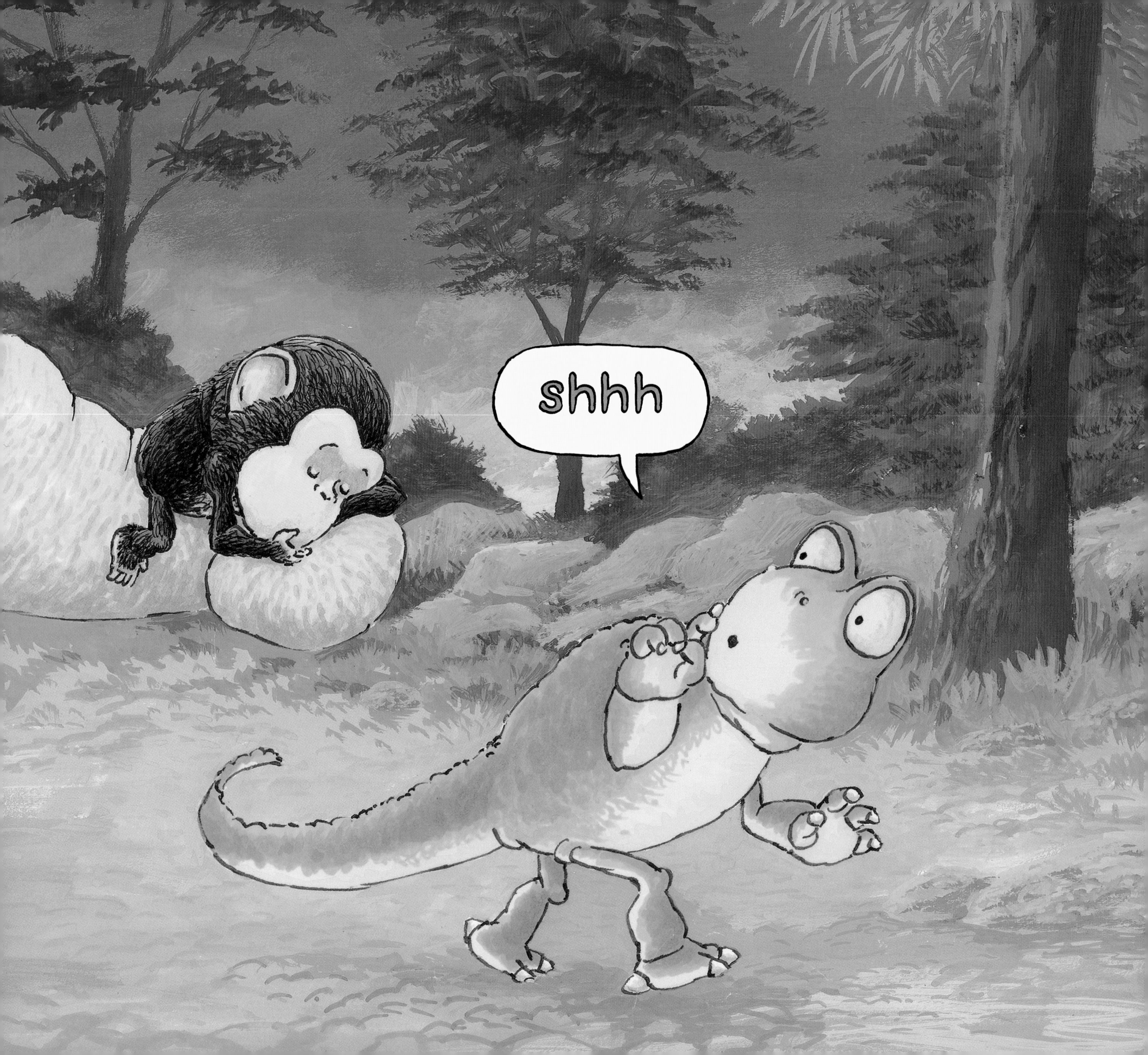
shhh

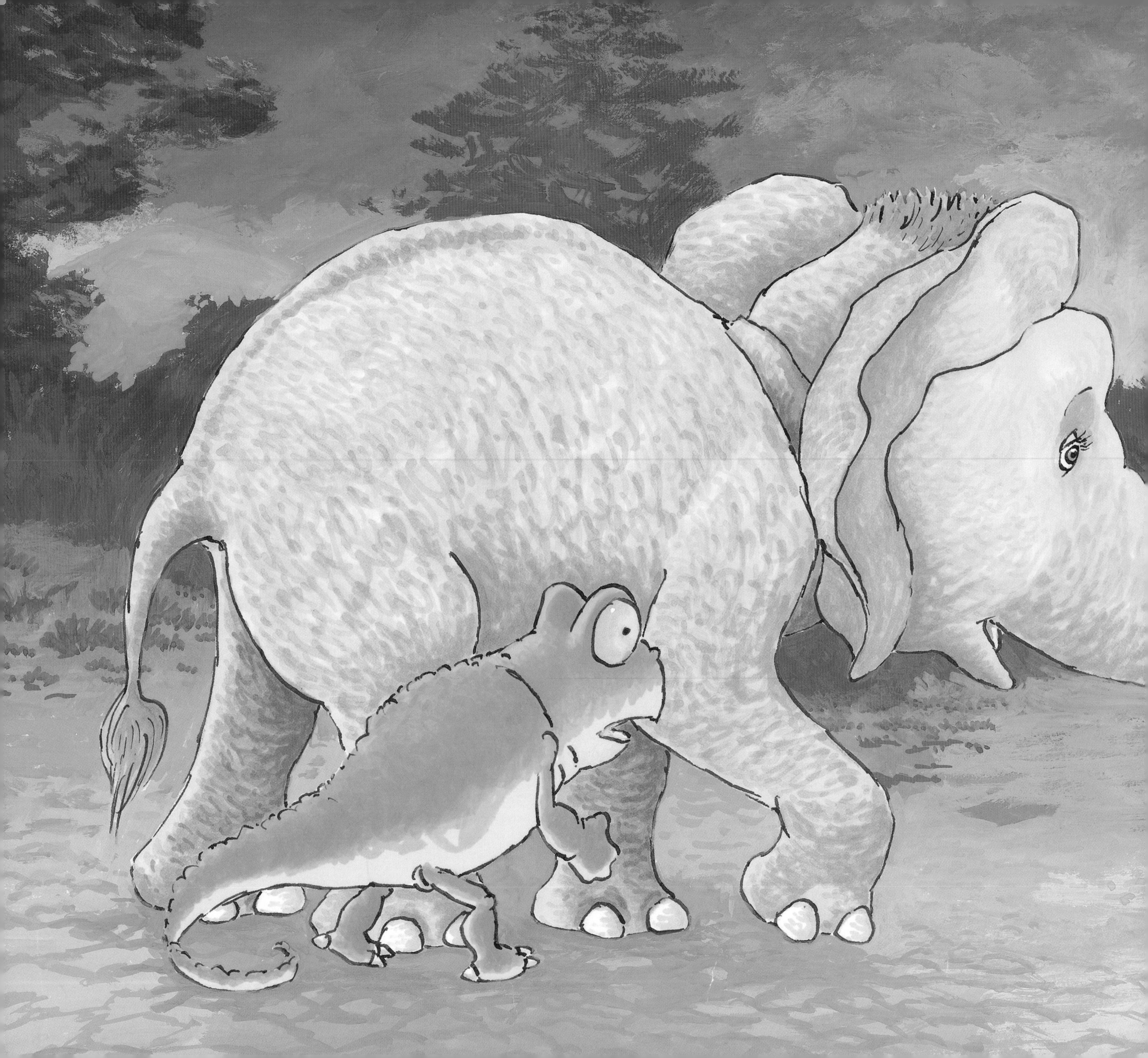

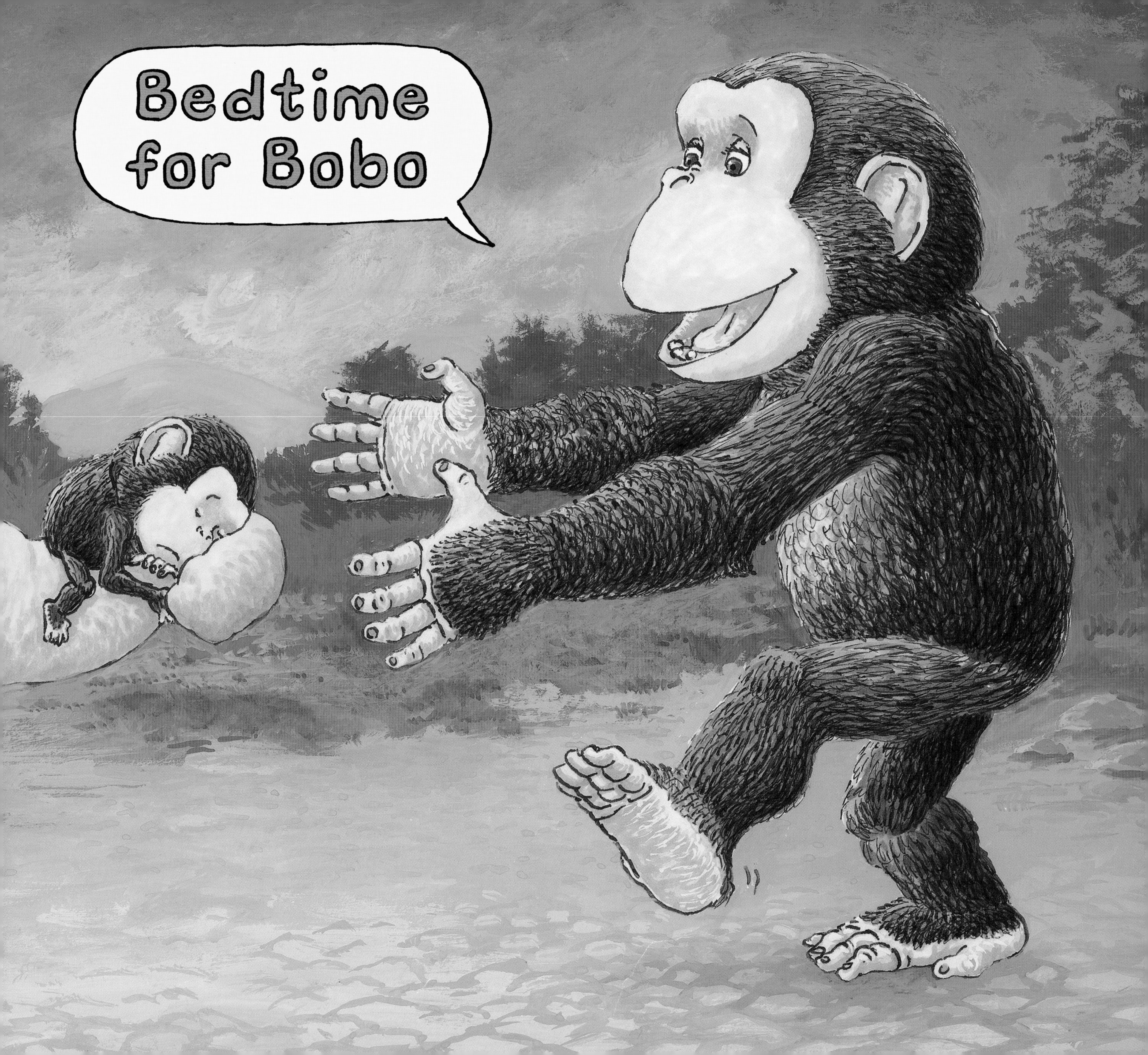
Bedtime for Bobo

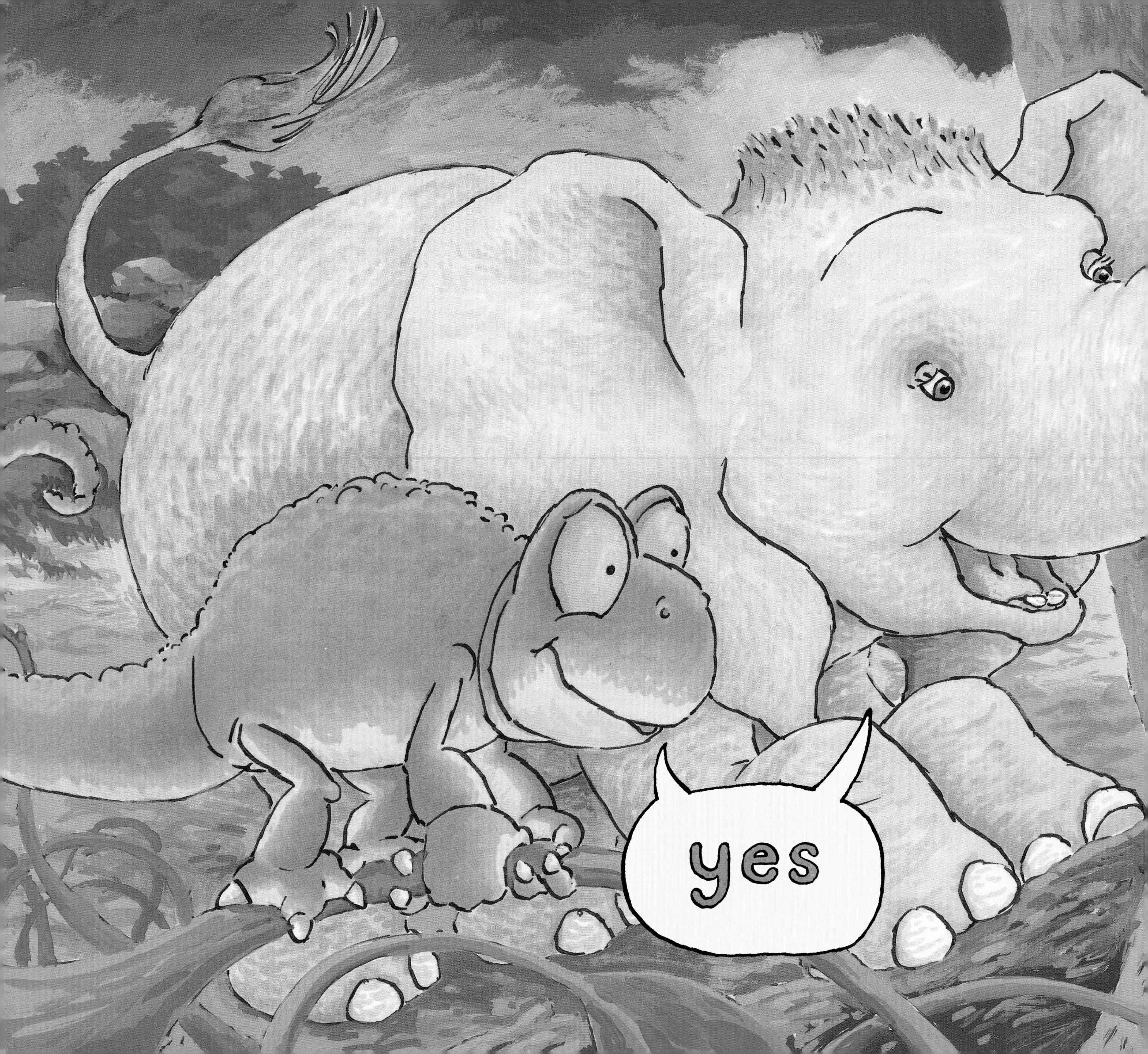
yes